AVERY'S BATTLEFIELD
—BOOK ONE—

Blessings

DEANNA K. KLINGEL

Deanna K. Klingel

journeyforth®

Greenville, South Carolina

Library of Congress Cataloging-in-Publication Data
Klingel, Deanna K.
  Avery's battlefield / Deanna K. Klingel.
    p. cm.
  Summary: Fourteen-year-old Quaker Avery Bennett has learned much from his mother about treating wounds and illnesses, and when he and his dog Gunner head into the Civil War battlefields in search of his Uncle Fredric in 1862, he finds many who need his help.
  ISBN 978-1-60682-171-8 (perfect bound pbk. : alk. paper)
  [1. Quakers—Fiction. 2. United States—History—Civil War, 1861-1865—Fiction. 3. Medical care—History—19th century—Fiction. 4. Dogs—Fiction. 5. Virginia—History—1775-1865—Fiction.] I. Title.
  PZ7.K6799Av 2011
  [Fic]—dc22
                                                          2010044148

Cover photos: Craig Oesterling (Young Man); iStockphoto.com © photoGartner (Dog Beagle), © DenGuy (US Civil War Artillery Firing), © warrengoldswain (boom!), © jimveilleux (Smoke Plume), © JudiLen (Forest fire), © molotovcoketail (classic banners), © hairballusa (Divided We Fall), © friendlydragon (confederate flag)

Design and page layout by Nick Ng

© 2011 by BJU Press
Greenville, South Carolina 29614
JourneyForth Books is a division of BJU Press

Printed in the United States of America

ISBN 978-1-60682-171-8

15 14 13 12 11 10 9 8 7 6 5 4 3 2

*Dedicated to those who choose
to do the hard thing,
because it's the right thing to do.*

Table of Contents

1861 JOURNEY OF A LIFETIME
PART ONE

1862 CITIES OF WAR
PART TWO

Acknowledgements

My sincere thanks and gratitude to

Larry Butler, my steering committee of one, who started me on this journey.

Brett Brubaker and David Ford, who embraced the story from the start.

Dr. Roberta Butler, PhD, for hours of reading, editing, and patient tutoring.

Cashiers' Writers Group for listening, critiquing, and encouraging.

Chris Godsey, school media specialist; Sarah Pichette and Dr. Sandra Hartman, PhD, for their editing skills; and Eli Klingel for his young perspective.

Tom Pierson for use of his Civil War library.

And thanks to many friends and family who shared from their areas of expertise:

Dr. Steven Lazoff, medical resources; Col. Albert Busck,Ret., all things military; Carole Clark and Ann McLeod for historical artifacts; Wendy Ricci, education on Gypsy Vanner horses; Jeff and Laurie Klingel for honey bee education and historical Virginia agriculture.

To my husband Dave, for computer skills and patience beyond the call of duty.

Thank you to Nancy Lohr, editor, JourneyForth Books, for patient encouragement and many prayers during revision.

Thanks to JourneyForth Books for taking on this project of my heart.

Many, many gracious thanks to all of you. This book wouldn't have made it out of the first draft without your encouragement.

PART ONE

JOURNEY OF A LIFETIME

1861

CHAPTER ONE

HOME FRONT

The early morning sunlight forced itself between the cracks of the loft walls where fourteen-year-old Avery Junior Bennett lay sleeping. He squeezed his eyes tighter and slid deeper under the quilt, ignoring the cracks of light and denying the smell of hash and eggs wafting from below in his mother's kitchen. Avery rolled over and sat up, cracking his skull on the sloping loft roof.

"Ow! When did I grow this tall?" He rubbed his head and offered his hurried morning prayers. He scrambled down the loft ladder in his long nightshirt and his woolen stockings. He jumped off the bottom rung and plunked himself down at the table.

"Morning, Mother." She smiled at him and spooned eggs and hash onto his plate. He helped himself to a piping hot biscuit and slathered it with butter and honey. Catching his mother's glance, he put the biscuit on his plate and bowed his head.

"Thanks be to God for all we are about to partake. And thank Thee for my mother too," he added, just for good measure before devouring his delicious, hot breakfast. Two empty coffee mugs sat on the table, and Avery knew his father and his brother, Clayton, were already at their chores. He washed his face and hands at the pump, grateful that his father had put a new pump indoors in the kitchen next to the stove. Warm water was something to be truly grateful for. He put on clean underclothes, shirt, britches, and knitted stockings. He plunked down on the kitchen chair and tugged on his boots.

He slid off the chair, unbolted the door, grabbed his coat, and went into the yard to begin his morning chores. Even the smallest chore was important on a farm, and now that he was fourteen, Father would be expecting even more of him.

He took a bowl of scraps and oatmeal into the barn for his best friend, Gunner, the best hound dog in the Kanawha Valley. Gunner, who'd been up since dawn, was happy to see him; and with his tail waving merrily, he ran circles around his young master. Avery filled the food trough with oats for his father's matched pair of draft horses and scattered corn for the chickens. He fed his own horse, Fan, and lingered to caress her strong neck. His brother was raking the barn floor, and his father was making some fence repairs.

"Morning." He waved to them.

"Happy birthday," they replied.

"Thank you."

Though birthdays were usually ordinary workdays and the Bennetts didn't spoil their boys, Avery always enjoyed his birthdays. His birthday was the first day of the first month, which he thought was a fine way to start a new year. Last evening he received a warm hunting coat with large game pockets. *That's a pretty grown-up gift*, he thought. The year before, he'd been given his own musket. His father had trained him for several years and believed he was ready for a hunting gun of his own. Three years ago his father gave him a hound puppy. Being certain that the pup would grow up to become a great gun dog, Avery named him Gunner.

Avery quartered some logs, brought them in, and piled them next to the stove. He pumped a bucket of water from the outside pump and brought it inside for cooking.

"Guess I'll be going over to help Mr. Sadler now," he called to his father. "Gunner, come."

"Yes, good; give Mr. Sadler my regards. I've laid some tools out for you in the shed. I appreciate your going for me; I really want to get this fence repaired today."

It was a good day to be outside, warm for this time of year. It was a day that held the promise that springtime was coming early to the hillsides of the hollers in Kanawha Valley. Buds were already beginning to swell, and the roads were alternately slushy and frozen.

Old Mr. Sadler had a lot of trouble with his arthritis, and at the church last Sunday he'd asked for help with some repairs. Avery took a long hank of rope from the tool shed, in case he needed to go onto the roof, and gathered the other tools his father had laid out for him. He saddled Fan, whistled for Gunner, and the three of them headed cross-country over the hill into the next holler.

They trotted up the hill, feeling as strong and fresh as the day itself. Fan delighted in the wind blowing through her mane and snorted happily. Gunner was challenged to keep pace as he kept stopping to take in all the exciting scents. At the top of the hill, they surveyed the vista while they caught their breath. Avery noticed the slushy snow melting slowly down the hillside on the sunnier side of the hill. They picked their way carefully down the hill. As they neared the bottom of the hill, Avery spotted Gunner standing at complete attention; his ears and tail were on alert. "Found yourself a rabbit to chase, did you?" But Gunner didn't chase. He sniffed the air and gave a low whine.

"What is it, boy?" Avery instinctively reached for his musket, but it was at home hanging on its pegs on the gun rack. Avery watched Gunner. It was clear that something had his attention.

"Gunner, find it." The dog took off bellowing straight to the edge of Miller's Pond in the distance; and Fan galloped off, following Gunner. At the pond's edge the hound's braying changed to a bark. Avery thought he was hearing something too. Gunner ran circles, barking, at the edge of the pond until Avery commanded him to shush. He quieted and looked intently at Avery. In the silence Avery heard a small voice calling from a distance. He ran to the edge of the melting ice.

A week ago he could have walked across this pond, but the last few warmer days had taken away that option. A thin layer of water lay across the ice. Where was the voice coming from? Gunner would know.

Avery called out, "Where are you?"

"Here! I'm— I'm he-here!" The little voice was sobbing.

"Gunner, show me." Gunner turned and stared across the pond at the far side.

Avery followed his stare. He could see that a large tree had fallen at the edge of the pond, probably during a storm last fall; it was frozen into the ice.

"Gunner, find it." The dog sniffed the air again and ran around the pond toward the tree.

Behind the fallen tree a hand was waving a stick in the air.

"We see you. What's your trouble?"

"I'm st-stuck in the w-water an' I-I'm c-cold. H-hurry." The little voice sounded terrified.

"Gunner, go." Avery and Fan ran around the end of the pond after Gunner, who was closing in on the tree, baying as he ran.

"We're coming, don't worry," he yelled. But when he got to the tree, he realized he'd been deceived by the appearance. The tree wasn't at the water's edge, it was across the pond. Clinging to the tree in a hole in the ice was a child in serious trouble. *How long had he been hugging the tree? Couldn't have been long or he'd be frozen already*, Avery reasoned.

Avery stepped cautiously onto the ice; the entire surface shifted. He sucked in a breath, and he said a quick prayer for guidance and wisdom; he tried to reassure the terrified child, who shivered and whimpered. He grabbed the hank of rope from his saddle, tied one end to Fan's bridle, and gave the other end to Gunner.

"Take it." Gunner obediently took the rope and looked at Avery, waiting.

"Go, Gunner." Gunner padded lightly across the wet ice.

"I-I g-got it," called the weak little voice. "M-my foot's st-stuck," he shivered. The little voice was sobbing and coughing.

Avery took hold of the rope tied to Fan, the other end being held by the child, and began to walk gingerly out on the ice.

When the ice shifted, he stood still, breathless; Gunner worried and whined. Avery proceeded a little farther, holding the rope in case he should fall through the ice. Gunner's ears were up, and he stared at Avery intently.

"I'm almost there; hold on, and don't give up. Hold onto the rope." He was almost to the tree. He held his breath and took the last step.

"Please, God," he prayed, "help us." He reached the tree and looked down into the hole on the other side. There was the child with a knitted woolen hat on his head, a pasty white face, and blue lips. His eyes were dazed. He was trying to hold Gunner's rope, but his numb fingers were uncooperative.

"How is your foot stuck?" He tried to look into the hole, but the water was black.

"I dunno." The sobbing little voice was getting weaker.

"How far can you climb out onto the tree?"

"Only this m-much."

Avery tried to reach down into the hole, but he could just reach the water. Gunner paced and whined sensing the danger. Avery climbed over the tree and lowered himself into the hole beside the child. He gasped as the cold took his breath away. His chest was squeezed by the frigid water; his lungs ached. He felt the child's body; it was very cold. He felt down the body to the legs. He followed one leg all the way to the foot. It was cold and stiff. He felt the other leg and followed it down until he felt strong branches at cross angles at the ankle. The foot was wedged between them.

"Can you wiggle your foot?" Avery was shaking with the cold. He noticed that the child wasn't shivering as much as he had been. *That's not good*, he thought.

"I can't feel my feet." The child sounded sleepy.

"Okay, don't worry. Stay awake. You have to help me now. We'll both get out of here, okay?" Avery's teeth chattered.

"Uh-huh." The little voice sounded far away, and the stocking cap was sliding down over his eyes.

Gunner paced and whined as Avery disappeared again.

Avery tried to open his eyes under the water, but under the shadow of the tree the water was dark, and it was so cold his inner ears screamed in pain. He tried to turn the child's foot first this way and then that way. He tried to move one of the branches, but it was frozen in place. He surfaced, drew a breath, and went under again. This time he pointed the toe downward, straightening out the foot; it fit between the branches.

He surfaced. "That's it!" Gunner barked his relief.

"I got it. Stay awake now; we're almost out." He shook the frozen child firmly. The child blinked and sucked in a breath. Avery went back under and quickly bent the foot and pushed it upward into the tight space between the limbs. He surfaced and was relieved to hear the child crying out in pain.

"Good, good. We're almost there." Under the water again he pulled up on the child's leg. The child screamed; Avery heard it under the water. The foot was free; Avery surfaced. But the child had let go of the tree and the rope, and panicking he splashed about in the water, frozen and fearful.

"Gunner, get the rope." Gunner picked up the rope that the child had dropped and brought it to Avery. He released the rope and dropped it into the hole. Avery picked it up and tried to give it to the floundering, terrified youngster. The child grabbed at Avery, choking with fear and slashing through the water.

"Stop! Take the rope." But the child seemed to not hear him. Avery knew that the boy was losing consciousness.

Gunner dropped to his elbows over the hole and snagged the little jacket with his teeth, holding the child's head above the water.

Avery wrapped the rope around the child's waist, tied it, and with Gunner pulling the jacket, Avery lifted the boy out of the water and laid him over the tree.

"Fan! Fan, back up," he hollered to Fan. He wished he had Father's draft horse that was used to backing in her daily work. Fan wasn't often asked to do this, and she was hesitant, uncertain of what she was being asked to do.

"Back up, Fan," he pleaded. "Please back up." He mumbled

numbly to himself, shivering wildly in the January sunshine.

Gunner ran gingerly across the ice to the horse and stopped in front of her. When she lowered her head to nuzzle him, he began to bark. The startled horse took a step back, and the dog continued to bark and bark, moving toward the horse. The horse began to back up, and the rope pulled taut. Avery grabbed the child and lowered him over the tree and carefully onto the ice. Gunner barked; Fan backed up; and the small victim was dragged across the ice.

Avery grabbed the tree and tried to pull his own body out of the water. Once he had the tree, he tried to wrap his legs around it and pull himself to the ice. His muscles were so cold he had difficulty telling his body what to do. Fan pulled the child to the edge of the pond. Avery dragged himself on his belly carefully across the pond to the shore. His hands burned and his fingers were numb.

Gunner was already there, lying across the child. He wagged his tail and gave a happy bark when Avery staggered toward them. *What now?* Avery tried to think. His mind was cloudy, and he wasn't thinking clearly. He needed to come up with a plan. "God, what should I do?"

He was shivering uncontrollably. He needed to warm this child—and himself.

Gunner went to Fan and started barking at her.

"Good idea, Gun." He staggered over to Fan and pulled at her bridle. He clucked, pressed his knee against her leg, and she bent her knees, going down on the ground.

"Good girl." He was moving slowly and thinking even slower. His insides quivered; he needed to hurry. When he turned back to look, Gunner was again lying across the trembling child. Avery tugged at the child, who murmured something, which he didn't understand. He tucked the child alongside Fan's belly. Gunner came and lay down beside the child.

Avery pulled his winter jacket off Fan's saddle, where he'd put it when he'd gotten too warm. Was that really just a few minutes ago? He took off his frozen shirt and put on the jacket that was warmed by the sun. He buttoned it up and laid himself down on top of his horse and dog in the sunshine. *We've made a child sandwich*, he thought dully to himself. How long did they warm? He had no idea. The sun was still warm when the youngster began to cry.

He talked to the child, who was still cold, but was now able to move. The boy wasn't so frightened anymore, and Avery needed to get some information from him. "Do you live nearby? How did you get here? Did you walk from home? How close is it? Do you know the way home? What's your name?" The information was slow and unclear, delivered with sobs around the thumb in the mouth.

When the child seemed to be warm enough to be out of danger, Avery got Fan up. He put the child on the saddle and swung up behind him. He wrapped his winter coat around the boy and pulling it tightly around the two of them, he buttoned it back up, holding the victim snugly next to him so they could share the body heat gathering inside the jacket.

They were away from the pond, and back on the cross-country track that Avery had been on just a short time ago. If nothing else, he'd take him to the Millers', which was only a few minutes away.

"Do you know how to find your home from here?" Avery asked. "What is your name? Don't you know your name?"

Finally, after a long hesitation, the little raspy voice said, "Tater McDougal."

"What? You're a tater? You're a McDougal?" He studied the woolen stocking cap. If he'd seen a mop of red hair, he would've known immediately that the child was one of the taters. "Then I know where you live. Why didn't you tell me?"

"I'm going to be in big trouble," said Tater. Avery turned Fan around and cantered to the McDougal's. He rode swiftly up their lane and was unbuttoning the jacket when Sam McDougal appeared at the side of the house.

Sam McDougal and his wife, Molly, lived on their potato farm. Sam called her "Me Angel Molly," and she called him "Me

Darlin' Sam." Sam and Molly's parents, God rest their souls, as Sam always said, came to this valley several years ago to escape the Great Potato Famine in Ireland. Sam and Molly met here, married, and raised potatoes, which they sold and traded to everyone in the valley.

Whenever they came to church, all the McDougals said their prayers quietly. "It's just our way," they explained, and they were welcomed among the worshippers. Avery never really talked to them other than to say a polite good morning. He was never certain exactly how many McDougal children there were. Sam said it was his "best row of 'taters." So every McDougal child, recognized by a mop of curly red hair, was called "Tater" by all the neighbors. Avery wondered if anyone knew all their names, or if, indeed, they had names.

"Mr. McDougal," Avery said, "I've got one of your taters here. He was in a bit of a fix, but I've gotten him warmed up a bit. He needs something hot for his innards and some dry clothes. He was nearly frozen to death and very scared."

Mr. McDougal went to Fan and lifted the child down in his arms. He wrapped his arms tightly around the cold tater and kissed the pale face.

"Oh me darlin'," cooed the father. "Come in, Avery, do. We've a nice warm fire a'goin'." Avery went into the house, and Mrs. McDougal came running into the kitchen.

"Oh, me baby, me sweet, sweet heart. Are you okay then?" She cupped the child's face in her hands and smothered it with kisses. She took the youngster to dry off and get warm clothes.

Mr. McDougal put the tea kettle on the fire. "You look a bit cold and damp yourself, lad."

"Sir, do you suppose I could borrow some dry clothes? I can return them cleaned on Sunday. But I'm pretty cold in these." He was still shivering, but his mind was clear.

So Avery, in dry clothes, warmed himself with the hot tea while he explained to Mr. McDougal what had happened; Gunner lay under the table.

"Thank ya, Avery Junior Bennett," Sam said. "Our family

is beholden to ya, lad."

"I'm just happy I was there."

"God sent ya there, don't ya know that for sure?"

"Mr. McDougal, I'm just a little curious. Why was the little tater all alone at Eli Miller's pond on the other side of your holler? Seems a long ways from home for such a little one."

"Aye, 'tis a ways. On the way headed to Miller's place, I 'spect. Rachel Miller is lyin' in, and she's two small ones already. Our older girl has gone there to help out. This little tater, whenever she gets into a fix, always runs to her sister for comfort. She was getting into a peck of trouble today, she was, and couldn't face it without her sister."

"*Her* sister? This tater is a *girl?*"

"Oh, yes." Molly McDougal had just come into the kitchen, carrying a little bundle of tea toweling. "This little tater is our darlin' Colleen."

Avery was so astonished he was speechless. It never occurred to him that this was a little girl.

"Colleen? That's her name? Hmm." *So the tater does have a name.* "And she was in trouble today?"

Molly McDougal laid the towel bundle on the table and unrolled it. On the towel lay a big pile of what looked like red banty rooster feathers. It took Avery a moment to figure out what he was looking at. Mr. and Mrs. McDougal burst into laughter. They laughed so hard they held their sides and landed in each other's arms for support. Avery realized then that he was looking at a heap of red curls. The girl had chopped off all her hair. He remembered the woolen stocking cap. He joined in the laughter. He drank a second cup of hot tea and finished his story of the icy rescue. Mrs. McDougal got very serious when she took Avery's arms and kissed his cheek.

"We've only got seven little taters and so have none to spare. Thanks to you we won't be losing one today. Thank ya, darlin' Avery."

"You're welcome. I really should go now. I'm on my way to help Mr. Sadler with some repairs."

A little voice came from around the door. "Ta, Avery."

He looked behind him. There was the little red haired tater in her warm nighty and dry stockings. Her mother's warm shawl was around her shoulders. With the stocking cap off and the color returning to her cheeks, Avery now recognized her as the little tater he'd seen on Sundays at the meeting house off and on since she was a baby. He guessed her age to be about six years. She was the little one with the shiny red hair in long tubular curls. She usually wore a big bow on the back to hold the curls in place. Now those curls lay on the table, looking like a pile of feathers. In places her scalp nearly showed through, and in the front the hair was cut right to her forehead. In some places, it was so short that the hair stood up straight. Her ears peeked out on both sides. Avery had to smile as he admired her handiwork.

"Ta, Avery," she said again.

"You're welcome, Colleen."

She spotted Gunner under the table and crawled on her knees across the floor and under the table. "Ta, Gunner doggy."

Avery peeked under the table to see the little girl's arms wrapped tightly around Gunner's neck and the dog nuzzling her cheek and ear. A little giggle escaped; Avery smiled at her.

"Gunner says you're welcome. You know the good thing about hair, Colleen? It grows back. Don't worry; it'll all be fine."

Avery arrived at Mr. Sadler's wearing Sam McDougal's pants mended several times, too short, too wide, and a shirt too long.

"Well, I declare, Avery, you sure growed out of those britches. You got a pair of long legs, that's for sure!" Old Mr. Sadler laughed and hobbled off the porch anxious for Avery to get to work.

His mother thought the same thing when he arrived home later, until she realized they weren't Avery's britches at all. Gunner sniffed the clothing repeatedly, knowing they didn't smell like Avery's clothes.

"Well, this looks like a good tale for supper," his mother said.

In spite of the humility with which he told the story, there was no doubt in anyone's mind that Avery, Gunner, and Fan were heroes. His father patted him on the back, and Clayton grinned at him. They all thanked God graciously for Colleen's rescue.

After supper dishes were washed up, his mother began sewing a little bonnet to give to tater Colleen at the meeting house on Sunday. If Avery described her deed properly, the child would surely be in need of one.

CHAPTER TWO

TROUBLE'S COMING

It was early spring; the soil was warming, and the farmers were busy sharpening their tools and planning for planting. The winter was nearly over, and the neighbors were beginning to get out again and call on each other. So Avery wasn't too surprised when he saw someone riding up the lane one sunny morning.

"Who could this be, Gunner?" Avery didn't think he knew anyone who rode a donkey. Gunner was interested and started out to greet the visitor. The rider wore a wide straw hat. Skinny legs in loose britches straddled the little donkey. The droopy straw hat covered most of his head and face. He wore a farm boy's barn coat. Avery wandered out to the yard to greet their visitor.

"Good day."

The visitor slid off the donkey, splashing into the mud, and held out a handful of little purple violets.

"Well, go on, take them; they're not poisoned, and they're the very first ones up."

"Huh?" *Who is this?* He reached out and took the little bouquet, studying the face of the visitor. The stranger suddenly yanked off the straw hat, and, with a shake of the head, a cascade of wild red curls unfurled around her pale face. She had a light sprinkling of sunny freckles on her nose.

"I just wanted to say thank ya for savin' me baby sister. Me mam told me about you."

"You're a tater then," he stammered shyly. "You're a Mc-Dougal."

"Aye, I'm a tater. I got me another name though, if you happen to be wonderin' about that. I'm Claire, Claire Ann McDougal." She stuck her hand out like a boy. "Nice to meet you," she said. "I've seen you on Sundays."

"Claire," he swallowed. He didn't know what else he should say. *Should he shake her hand?* Well, she was waiting; okay, he shook her hand. She'd seen him on Sundays? He felt his ears tingling. She knew him? She'd noticed him? He stared and blushed. How had he missed seeing her?

"Claire. Nice name," he said, tripping over his tongue.

"Well, it's polite manners to state your name, you know; but I already know you to be Avery, so never ya mind. Thank you for all of it, my sister and all," she said confidently.

Before he could think of an answer, she grabbed his arms, stretched to her tip toes, and planted a big kiss on his cheek. The amazed boy dropped the violets and gaped. She hopped onto the little donkey, straddling it like a boy, while shoving her hair back into the straw hat. She touched the donkey with her heels and trotted back down the lane. Avery was rooted to the spot. He touched his cheek.

Standing on the porch, Clayton smiled. "I believe that was a sweet tater, huh, Avery?"

"I . . . well . . . I don't know; naw, I mean, I don't know about that. She's Claire, one of the taters."

"Uh-huh, a sweet tater who's sweet on Avery," his brother teased him. "Mmm-mm." Clayton's eyes twinkled.

Avery dismissed him with an angry wave of his hand and went back to his work in the shed, aware that his face and ears felt hot and prickly. He was sure they must be red; even redder now that he knew Clayton had watched this foolishness. He rubbed his kissed cheek and shrugged.

"She knew my name, Gunner. She saw me on Sundays. Is she nosy? Claire. That's a nice name; Colleen and Claire Ann. Hmm, how about that, Gunner? We know two taters by name."

The next Sunday Mother tucked the little bonnet into her bag to carry to the meeting house to give to Colleen McDougal. When they went out the door, they were surprised to see the horses already hitched and the wagon ready to go.

"What's this, Avery? Well, thank you. You're in a rush today. What's the occasion?" asked his father.

"This much eagerness for a Sunday meeting, huh, Avery?" Clayton, with a slight smirk on his face, studied Avery, whose face was growing redder.

"Well, it'll be nice to see all the neighbors, I suppose," Avery said. "I hope all the talking isn't going to be about war and fighting again this Sunday." He quickly changed the subject.

The talk of hostilities during those winter months had worried Avery. Many of the Virginians in the peaceful Kanawha Valley, like the Bennetts, were Quakers. Others were not. What they held in common was their faith in God, love of the soil, and their country. They shared their Sunday worship and a meal afterwards. For the farmers, it was their opportunity to catch up on the news: births, deaths, crops. A Wheeling newspaper was shared—whenever someone had one—with stories of impending rebellion; some reporters ventured to call it war.

"It's important to keep up with current affairs, Avery, even when it's not affecting us. We all believe in freedom, equality, and the Union of States; and though we won't take up arms, it's important that we know about it," his mother said.

"Many of our neighbors who immigrated from the Old Country believed they were so far away here in the United States they would be rid of rebellion and wars forever. But now, it seems, they might have been wrong," added his father.

"Really, Father? You think the war will come here?" Avery asked. His father didn't answer him, but clucked to the horses and drove silently.

The neighbors' unified prayer was for wisdom for President Lincoln and Jefferson Davis the new president of the Confederacy, that this might soon be over. But the old folks from the Old Country shook their heads and warned that this was just the beginning. "Trouble's coming," they said.

The farm women brought the last of their winter stores to share. They brought spring ramp salad, spring onion soup, and the last of the smoked venison and hams from winter. Hens were laying again, and Mrs. Mikesell brought her ginger cookies. Everyone had cleaned out their root cellars to prepare for the next season, so there was plenty to eat. The Bennett boys were hungry. Avery filled his plate and scanned the room from the corners of his eyes. Gunner watched him from under the table. Clayton studied him from across the table, smiling slightly.

"Looking for someone, Avery?"

"No, just eating." His red ears burned.

It was on this same day they learned from the newspaper that a Confederate force under General Beauregard fired on a U.S. military installation at Fort Sumter, South Carolina.

"That's an act of war," said Clayton excitedly. All the young men were in a state of agitation and argued the rest of the afternoon, sharing how they felt about this coming war. Avery moved between the adult men and Clayton's friends, listening to all sides. The State of Virginia, he heard, had responded by seceding from the Union and joining the Confederacy. The men shook their heads and murmured.

"Can't be," they said. "We're Virginians." One of the men slammed his fist into his palm.

"I think we will all soon be called upon to control our tempers and use reason," his father said. He put his hand on Avery's shoulder and gave it a little squeeze. "Tempers will soon flare," he said.

Avery thought about this all the way home. How could war come to this holler? What would that be like? Would it be scary? Would it change things for his family? He was feeling all out of sorts. His temper began to ruffle inside him. He felt like punching something. He clenched his fists and considered punching his brother. And then he remembered his father's words about that.

"One day, if you don't learn how to control your temper,

it'll land you in trouble," his father had told him. "Don't misunderstand me; anger isn't the problem. Many things that you see, hear, or experience in your life will make you rightfully, justifiably angry. But what you do with that anger will determine what kind of man you'll become. You must learn to manage your temper or it'll manage you, and it'll control your life. You have good reasoning, even at your age. And you're well-spoken for one so young, Avery. These gifts will grow, as you mature. And you must learn to use those gifts instead of your fists. You'll be able to change more things with reason and words than with fighting. That's our Quaker heritage, Avery. Think about what you could say or do to change the situation, other than punching. Words and reason; will you try?"

"Yes, Father." He'd been a youngster then, but his father's words guided him even now. Words and reason instead of fists. Avery unclenched his fists and gave Clayton a playful little cuff on the shoulder and smiled at him.

"George Maloney and Elmer Wyatt said they're going to meet up with an Ohio regiment that's camped near Grafton. They're ready to answer the President's call. The enlistment is only three months; they'll be back in time for summer harvest and fall planting. What do you say about all this, Father?"

"This rebellion doesn't involve us."

Avery tried to picture George and Elmer in uniform, carrying guns aimed at other men. It just wasn't a picture he could create. This was a peaceful valley where peaceful families live.

When they arrived home and the two brothers were putting up Father's horses, Avery reached out and held Clayton's sleeve.

"You thinking about George and Elmer?"

Clayton shrugged. "I have to give it some thought."

"But, Clayton—"

"I don't want to talk about it right now, okay? I have to think and pray about it."

"Yeah, sure." Gunner put his paw on Clayton's knee and whined. The boys laughed. "Gunner will pray with you, Clayton."

Clayton was quiet for a few days, and Avery wondered how long he would think about it before he brought it up to Father. Then one night at supper he did.

"Father, I believe this rebellion does involve us. We didn't go looking for it, but it's here."

"We're Virginians. We're on neither side of the unrest."

"Yes, we are Virginians. And that's why we must be heard. Virginia is a southern state, to be sure, but all of us aren't Confederates. Richmond's ways are not our ways. We need to support the Union of States. If no one stops this rebellion, the Union will cease to exist. You have read to us from the Bible that to rebel against authority is to rebel against God. Well, what does God say about rebelling against the United States?" Father laid his spoon down and looked at his oldest son.

"But, Clayton," Avery interrupted. His mother touched his arm and nodded, and Avery was silenced.

"You're a boy of seventeen, but you speak like a man. There's wisdom in what you say. But you're a peaceable Quaker; you can't take up arms against brethren. It's not our way." His father folded his hands. "Have you prayed about this, Clayton?"

"I have, Father. I've prayed for wisdom, strength, and charity. I believe that while it can never be right to take up arms against brethren, I think every man has a duty to defend what's important to him. A man can stand for something, or he can stand for nothing; I stand for the union of our country. I'd like to have your blessing, Father. I don't want to go against you, but I plan to leave tomorrow."

It seemed that all the air was sucked out of the room. His mother took in a short gasp. Avery watched her across the table as she laid her hand on her husband's shoulder. When it came to their sons, they spoke with one voice.

"I can't condone what you're doing, son. But a man must make his own decision in the matter of conscience. God bless you, and I'll pray that your service will be pleasing to God."

Avery had lost his appetite and didn't finish his supper. He lay awake half the night trying to imagine life without his brother beside him and life with war around them. He prayed for Clayton lying next to him in the loft.

When Avery awoke the next morning, the middle row of pegs on the gun rack was empty; Clayton was gone.

The beautiful springtime in the valley made it difficult for the farmers to visualize the skirmishes and bloodshed that were beginning to spread across the other states and in the rest of Virginia. Later that month while they were plowing and planting, the State of Virginia divided. The northwestern part, made up in good portion by the Kanawha Valley, rejoined the Union.

One afternoon, Avery's father received an urgent message by courier from Wheeling.

Greetings to my old friend and colleague.
These are troubling times for us, are they not?
I know you will not be taking up arms,
but I beg you to take up your pen and ink
and join us in Wheeling to determine the
future of the new State of Kanawha. Every
county in the western part of Virginia is
being asked to send five of their wisest men
to the Constitutional Convention in our new
capitol at Wheeling. Please join us as soon as
possible.
*   Sincerely, your old colleague,*
*   Francis H. Pierpont.*

"What shall I do, Sarah?" he asked his wife. "Pierpont wants me to come. But how can this be constitutional?" worried Avery's father. "If secession from the Union is unconstitutional, then how can secession from one's own state be anything else?"

"Perhaps," said his mother, "that's why they need wise men, to answer such questions of legality. You're a lawyer and a good one. This is how you're asked to serve. You must go. How can you not? Pierpont . . . your state . . . needs you."

"But how can I leave you here during such a time? What if—"

"Don't, Avery." His mother ended the conversation.

"Father, we will miss you, but we'll be fine," young Avery reassured his father.

Two days later Avery and his mother waved goodbye to Avery Bryson Bennett, former Boston lawyer, Virginia farmer, future delegate to the Congress of the new State of Kanawha. The top row of pegs on the gun rack was empty.

CHAPTER THREE

AUNT CAROLINE

Springtime washed over the Kanawha Valley with refreshing showers. Apple blossoms created white clouds of fragrance over the hillsides. Daffodils bloomed cheerfully on all the farms and bobbed their heads in the breeze. Calves bawled. The black earth smelled rich with promise, and the green beginnings of the summer crops peeked through the dirt in long, straight lines, organized, like the lives of these farmers, by the seasons. When the sun came out, a large rainbow seemed to begin and end in the Kanawha Valley. The fish were biting, and Avery had trouble keeping to his chores until they were finished properly. A bobwhite called plaintively from the field. Gunner's ears pricked up; he listened and paced impatiently.

It was on this auspicious day that Aunt Caroline arrived at their farm. She came by stagecoach, and then by train to Parkersburg where their neighbor Mr. Trotsky met her. Mr. Trotsky drove the wagon, which was piled high with her belongings that were tied down with rope.

Aunt Caroline, Avery's mother's younger sister, grew up in Boston; both were daughters of Dr. Clayton Littlefield, the best doctor in Boston. Aunt Caroline was a teacher at the Quaker Academy in Boston, but left to marry Uncle Fredric. And now here she was, alone at the Bennett farm.

She embraced her sister, hugged Avery, and scratched Gunner behind the ears. She looked around and breathed in the clean, fresh air.

"Well, I'm here," she said. Then she broke down in tears. His mother fixed some herbal tea and told her to sit down to tell what had happened, why she was here, and what was wrong.

"Avery," she instructed, "tend your chores and unload Caroline's things." Avery went out. He could tell Aunt Caroline was upset, and he wanted to hear their conversation. He moved around the wagon slowly and quietly, trying to eavesdrop through the open kitchen window.

"Fredric said I couldn't understand. And I don't!" Caroline cried harder. "Fredric is German, a Huguenot. His family came from Germany to Pennsylvania. But from there they moved to Charleston, South Carolina, where Fredric was raised. He never told me these things until recently. But I think Father guessed it, and that's why he was opposed to my marrying Fredric. Oh, if only I'd listened, I'd not be in this situation."

"And what situation is that, sister?"

"We owned a fine home in Boston," she sobbed. "It was in the best neighborhood, and Fredric was successful in his accounting business; I thought this would go on forever, I was so happy. Then this rebellion, this unrest, whatever it's to be called. Only then did I hear the rest of Fredric's story." She sniffed and wiped her tears on her handkerchief.

"He said it was so beautiful in Charleston, South Carolina, that I couldn't imagine it. His parents are too old to manage their holdings, he told me; and with the war—he actually said that, the *war*—approaching, he needed to return there. He said his heart belongs at River's Bend Plantation in Charleston and that Boston could never be his home. I thought Boston *was* our home. He said one day soon River's Bend would all belong to him."

"That all sounds wonderful. What are you doing here? Why aren't you with Fredric?"

"He went back to the rice plantation in Charleston to keep his slaves in line. Yes, Sarah, he's a slave owner. He and his family own hundreds of them. They have the largest rice plantation in the entire country. He never told me that before. He said they couldn't run the place without slaves. He's afraid they're getting restless with all this talk of setting slaves free, and some of them in South Carolina have tried to escape. Union gunboats on the river have stolen some of them from the rice fields and taken them north to freedom. Fredric went there to prevent this and to keep the slaves from escaping. He's hired someone to keep control of his slaves; someone with a firm hand he said. I heard them discussing this *control* in my own parlor, and it sickens me." She sobbed with anger and hurt. Sarah reached for Caroline's hands and held them tenderly, listening intently.

"How could I have fallen in love with a man who owns people and keeps them captive? How can I live with a man who is cruel and abusive to people? I can't, Sarah, I can't. And I thought we'd have such a good life together. It's over. I can't live there. I can't ever own other people. Fredric knew when we married that I was an abolitionist, and he deliberately kept this from me." She shook her head and broke down again. This time her sister didn't offer tea; she only hugged her.

"It turns out that his accounting business is all about buying and selling slaves for his plantation. Right there in Boston, under my very nose! He means to settle things at River's Bend, and then he's joining the army. He knows how I'd feel about that; he did it deliberately to hurt me." Her sad voice was barely audible and her tears were streaming down her cheeks. Sarah squeezed her sister's hands.

Caroline continued. "There's more. Our child is to birth in the fall. Oh, Sarah, I feel so betrayed." She cried as if her heart would break.

"Oh, Caroline, dear sister, I'm so sorry for you. But it isn't for us to judge Fredric Lennemann. God will do that. We must pray for his protection and pray for wisdom. This is going to be a trying year for all the citizenry of this country, and we may all be asked for some sacrifice. God help us all, I think this is only the beginning. You're welcome here; it's right that you should come to us." Sarah embraced her sister.

Avery unloaded her belongings, stored her few pieces of

furniture in the barn, corralled her little goat, and put her trunk in the house.

"What kind of a man would just go off and leave his wife like that, Gunner? Someone needs to go get him, tell him about his baby, and bring him home to Aunt Caroline. Someone should. Someone needs to talk some reason to the man. Looks like first the rebellion caused the Union to come apart, then it caused the State of Virginia to come apart, and now it's caused Aunt Caroline and Uncle Fredric to come apart," he said to Gunner. "What next? But it's good she's here. It's another set of hands to help with the chores and good company for Mother. Someone needs to find Uncle Fredric."

CHAPTER FOUR

AVERY'S DECISIONS

It was just about sundown when Avery heard the sound of horses riding hard down the post road. He read in the Wheeling newspaper about marauders who were stealing from the farms and doing other damage all in the name of the war effort, and he had a feeling this might be trouble. Avery quickly called to his mother and Aunt Caroline and told them to go into the bedroom, bolt the door, and stay out of sight.

"Watch me from the window, and you'll know what to do," he said. He didn't give them any time to argue, and calling Gunner to his side, he ran back to the privy. He snatched up Aunt Caroline's nanny goat grazing nearby and put her inside the privy with him. He told Gunner to lie down in front of the door and stay. He heard the horses charging across the yard, and he imagined that his heart was beating just as loud and as fast as their hooves. He hoped they would see Gunner first, and his plan would work. He heard one of them go into the barn, and he heard Fan whinny. Then he heard the coarse voice, and the privy shook when it was kicked.

"Hey, I know you're in there, come on out of there. We've come to *borrow* some things for the war effort. Come on out and do your duty."

"Okay," said Avery in a sickly, weak voice, "But you'll have to wait just a minute. I got the dysentery, and I'm really sick. We're all real sick around here; we all got dysenteries, and vomits, and all of it. Even my dog is sick; Gunner's about to die. Aren't you about to die, Gunner?" he called out. Gunner, on cue, rolled over on his back, put his feet in the air, and groaned, his best trick. The two women, catching on to Avery's plan, hung out the window and began to gag, retch, and moan.

The man by the privy ran off, calling to his partners to come on get out of there, or they'd all be sick with the dysentery. They took what booty they'd already sacked, the stock already tied to the wagon, and took off clumsily back to the post road.

When Avery was sure they'd gone, he came out of the privy, released his dog, thanked him, and hugged him, laughing partly with amusement, partly with relief. The two women came out of the house, doubled over in nervous laughter. They laughed and jostled each other around until they were all laughing behind the privy.

"Well played, Sister," laughed Aunt Caroline.

"I didn't know we were all such good actors."

"Good boy, Gunner." Avery rolled on the ground with his dog. Stopping to catch their breath, they all fell silent at the sight of a surprise vine loaded with squash blossoms that was growing up against the privy in the sunshine.

Looking out at the garden, through which the marauders had just raced their horses, they dropped to their knees and gave thanks for the squash, which might be all they had left.

"What have they done?" Mother gasped. "Our garden, oh, no," she cried and ran into the trampled field. They salvaged what they could of the small plants in the garden that would've been enough to feed them all through the summer and the next winter.

Avery took off for the barn. He ran to Fan's stall. It was empty. Gunner whined and came to his side, sniffing where his stall companion should be. The forlorn looking dog lay down in the straw.

"Fan," Avery whispered. He couldn't find his voice. He looked in his sad dog's eyes and knew he wasn't the only one who would miss Fan. He looked across the stall at his father's draft horses. One stall was empty. His father's matched pair had worked as partners all their lives. They were Father's prized horses; now one would pull alone.

"How could this happen?" Avery felt his stomach churning. He felt like he'd been kicked by a mule, the breath knocked out of him. His fists tightened. He was so mad; he was as mad as he'd ever been. He kicked the empty stall gate. He kicked Fan's stall. He grabbed the milk bucket and flung it across the barn.

"How could they do this to us?" he railed. He punched the empty feed bags; Gunner barked at him.

"They've ruined us. We should shoot them for this," he yelled, finding his voice. Gunner stared at him, barking and barking, trying to get his attention.

Avery dropped to the straw in Fan's stall and cried, pounding the floor. Gunner came to his side and sat vigilantly. Avery wrapped his arm around his dog and felt himself calming down.

"What'd I do, Gunner? I'm so mad. But I'm not mad at you. It's just my temper, and I'm so mad; what'll we do? I want to kill those marauders. That's a sin, isn't it? I know that. I promised Father I'd work at my temper." Gunner nuzzled Avery's cheek.

"Thanks, Gunner, I can always count on you." He wiped his eyes with the back of his hand, and his sobs quieted.

"Fan's your partner too; I know you're sad too."

Gunner whined in agreement.

"What'll we do? Oh, dear God, what'll we do? Tell me, God, what should I do?"

He lay still, trying to calm his anger and remembering his father's words until he heard the supper bell.

At supper the women thanked Avery for grabbing the nanny and putting her in the privy for safety. She'd now be their only source of milk, cheese, and butter; the cow was gone. Along with their oats and grain bags for the stock, the marauders had taken most of their staple supply that was stored in the spring house. Fan was gone, and one of Father's draft horses. Tools had rattled on down the road in the marauders' wagon. The family gave thanks for their own safety, as marauders had injured or killed farmers who had gotten in their way. It was a sad, quiet supper.

"How did you think of it, Avery?" Caroline asked.

"Clayton's last letter," he replied. "Clayton wrote that the soldiers' biggest fear wasn't the enemy; it was dysentery. So I figured to scare them. Guess that was a pretty good trick."

They all forced a little laugh at the joke and gave thanks for supper, good health, and safety. Inside, Avery's heart was aching for his horse. He prayed that she'd be kept well.

Sarah tried to sleep, wondering how the garden would recover, and if the plowing would be accomplished with half a team. The team was her husband's pride and joy; she hated to tell him.

Avery lay awake thinking about Fredric. *We need him back here. If he knew how sad Aunt Caroline was without him, and if he knew about his baby, he could change his thinking. Someone needs to fetch him.*

A few days after the marauders' visit, Avery found Mother and Aunt Caroline in the garden. He sat down between the rows of dirt and cleared his throat the way his father did whenever he wanted to say something important. The women looked up.

"I've been thinking about this a lot, and I've prayed about it too. I want to go find Uncle Fredric, tell him about his baby, and bring him home. We need him here. Gunner and I can do this; I know we can."

Both Mother and Aunt Caroline objected: *the war is starting, you are only fourteen, we need you here* . . . . But in the end, Avery won all the arguments.

"Just like his father," both the woman said. Avery was pleased with that idea.

A few days later when the morning sun bleached the night sky, Avery awoke. Today was the day he would leave to find Uncle Fredric. His heart raced to keep up with the butterflies twirling in his stomach. He folded his hands and said his morning prayers.

He dropped out of the loft and landed with a thump in the kitchen. He dressed hurriedly. He noticed that his boots were getting tight, and since he was wearing the new woolen stockings his mother had knitted for him, the boots were even tighter. He pushed and shoved and finally squeezed his feet into the boots, wondering how he'd pull them off that night. He milked the nanny goat. He shared a couple of poorly aimed squirts with the barn cat and laughed when her little black face was showered with milk.

"Good thing Aunt Caroline brought the little goat, since Betsy's gone," he told the cat. He took the pail of milk in to his mother and took a large bowl of scraps from last night's dinner out to the barn for Gunner. He filled the food trough for his father's lonely draft horse and sadly thought of Fan. He missed her, and he'd like to bloody the nose of that marauder who stole her. He threw down corn for the few remaining chickens, wondering how the marauding thieves had missed them. He finished his chores, and when he was satisfied with his wood pile and water buckets, he went inside.

He stood near the table and watched his mother busy with her tins, bottles, and jars. She carefully measured and filled them with her precious herbs, tinctures, salves, oils, and tisanes. He brought his knapsack to the table. He'd packed his few articles of clothing, a little tin of sewing supplies, and a larger tin box containing his mother's jars of medicines, rolls of bandages, and plasters. They rolled his wool blanket and filled a large gunny sack with food provisions. He and his mother had made hardtack all week in preparation for this trip. The little crackers served many dietary purposes without spoiling. Dried fruit, dried meat, root vegetables, and lots of hard tack would make up his meal staples for this journey.

Finally, she spoke. "Look at this canteen." She showed him a round, tin container with a pewter spout, and a blue fabric strap stamped with the official seal of the U.S. Army.

"Look inside here."

Avery peered inside the tin.

"This charcoal filter that I've fitted here in the center must remain tight. You see that?"

Avery nodded.

"You fill it with water here on the right side. To use the water, tilt it like this." She demonstrated. "The water passes through the filter. You see? Then you pour it out the left side over here. Do you understand?" Avery nodded. He wondered where she'd gotten this, but he wouldn't ask. He was always amazed at his mother's resourcefulness.

"Don't let anyone drink from your canteen, son. No one. If you wish to share your water, you pour it out for others. This is important. Fill your canteen only with clear, cold water from a waterfall, or water that you've boiled. Will you remember that? Don't drink any water from a pond or standing water, do you hear me?"

"Yes, Mother, I'll remember." Avery's mother believed in the importance of clean water. Many people in the Kanawha Valley thought she was too fervent about her matter of cleanliness, but since she never got sick, folks listened to her advice. Some of the neighbors thought she was a bit bossy, but if one of their family members took ill, it was always Sarah Littlefield Bennett they sent for. She knew all about medicines. Well, at least more than anyone else. Avery had grown up with clean hands, clean finger nails, and clean water.

They packed a small Bible in the knapsack along with a cooking pot, tinder, fire starters, and sulfur matches. He put a chunk of lye soap into a woolen stocking and tied the stocking to the knapsack, where it dangled. The rolled wool blanket was placed on top of the knapsack. They wrapped the entire thing tightly in an India rubber sheet. Over that they wrapped an oil cloth; it was all tied neatly and tightly with rope. A small hatchet and his Bowie knife in its leather sheath hung from the rope. He tucked his treasured journal and writing tools in his inner jacket pocket.

Mother slid bracelets onto Avery's wrists and tied a larger one around Gunner's neck. She made these bracelets out of long narrow pockets of fabric which she filled with penny royal, thyme, and wormwood to keep the fleas from bothering them. He'd packed this way many times to go on hunting trips with his father and camping with his brother, Gunner, and Fan. This time, it was just he and Gunner. He thought longingly of his riding companion, Fan.

"We'll both be missing Fan, won't we, Gunner. She should be here."

Realizing that his time of departure was near, his stomach fluttered nervously. He put on his hunting coat and placed a carefully folded map and a compass in the pocket. Yesterday he'd painstakingly copied this map of Virginia from his father's treasured atlas. He put some powder and shot in one of the large pockets, and took his musket from the bottom pegs on the gun rack that hung on the wall. He paused and looked at the top pegs where his father's Kentucky rifle should be; it was gone. His brother's musket that hung on the second row was missing. And now the bottom row where his belonged was also empty.

He hugged his mother; she hugged him long and hard. She whispered a few words and stepped back, tears pooling in her eyes. Aunt Caroline hugged him and assured him of her prayers.

"God go with thee," his mother said. He stepped through the door, whistled for Gunner, and walked across the yard toward the post road. Gunner bounded to his side. Avery knew his mother was in the kitchen beseeching God to keep her boy well and safe. He was happy that Aunt Caroline was with her.

Walking up the farm lane now with his map and compass, dog and knapsack, Avery was hoping and praying that he'd be up to the task. His father had taught him to control his temper, hunt, fish, to look folks in the eye, and use good manners. His mother had taught him to cook, stay healthy, and use medicines properly. They had both taught him to read, write, and factor; he knew some history and geography. Frequently his mother would say, 'Here's a knowledge point for you, Avery.' Then she'd tell him a fascinating fact about something, and they talked about it. He always remembered the knowledge points and wrote them in his journal along with new words he learned. He would miss his mother while he was gone, that was a fact he knew for sure. But what did he really know of Virginia beyond Kanawha? He gave a little shudder and uttered a prayer for courage to face the unknown. He had no idea where he was going or how long it would take; his young heart was fearful but excited.

CHAPTER FIVE
THE TURNPIKE

Avery and Gunner walked up their lane to the post road and headed for Parkersburg to the train station. From Parkersburg they'd take the train to Grafton, where men were enlisting. Then they'd walk to the Parkersburg-Staunton Turnpike, asking along the way, heading east. Surely someone in Virginia would've met Uncle Fredric.

Avery was glad he only had a short trip on the steamy, smoky train. The seats were scratchy; it was hot and crowded, and it smelled like a chamber pot. He was too excited to sleep, too crowded to enjoy looking out the window, and too claustrophobic to remain here for long. He picked up a newspaper that was left behind by one of the passengers and read it. It was filled with stories and drawings of the rebellion.

"Is this how the war looks?" He looked at the drawings in amazement.

"Grraafftton" called out the conductor, and Avery and Gunner disembarked into the sunshine. He'd been to the Grafton train station before, but he'd never seen it so crowded.

Men were everywhere, pushing through the crowds, arguing, pointing, and debating. He read the broadsides all around him pasted on the station walls and on all the other buildings. The broadsides instructed the men where to go to enlist in the service of the U.S. Army for three months or where to go to join the Confederate forces. Fist fights broke out around the station as each faction tried to pull down the other's broadsides. Soldiers moved in and out of the crowd, and roughnecks looked for a fight.

"Let's get out of here, Gunner," he said, and he meant it. He took out his compass. With a silent prayer they walked off in the direction that he hoped was toward the Parkersburg-Staunton Turnpike, where they'd begin their journey eastward to find Uncle Fredric. He walked along the turnpike talking to Gunner, mumbling to himself, and praying to God.

"What would get into a man's head to make him take off and leave his wife and his job like Uncle Fredric did, huh, Gunner? Father always said that when you make a commitment, you live with it. Uncle Fredric decided to marry Aunt Caroline and make a family, and then he up and quit. I say we bloody his nose, Gunner, how about that?"

Gunner tilted his head and looked sideways at Avery, showing the white of his eye. Avery laughed out loud and skipped a stone down the road.

"Just seeing if you're paying attention."

It was getting into summer now, and some of the days were warm and humid. Avery and Gunner walked on through the pretty valley. Avery cut the toes out of his boots to allow his toes some room.

"Ah, this feels better," he said, wiggling his toes. His britches didn't reach his boots any more. But he kept himself clean and said his prayers regularly. He and Gunner ate only what they needed. He camped off the road and was amazed that they were faring so well. He occasionally passed a post rider, and he waved in the friendly valley manner. Whenever he had an opportunity, he inquired about Fredric Lennemann.

Some days they heard gunfire off in the distance. A few times he saw smoke rising over the hills, too great to be a cooking fire. He watched from the trees one morning as a company of Confederate soldiers passed by. He was awed by their numbers.

"Gunner, I don't think we have this many men in all of Kanawha Valley. This is like watching a long train passing by." He and Gunner lay on their bellies along the turnpike, peering out from under the shrubbery and tall weeds.

One humid, cloudy day Avery realized he had no idea what day it was or even what month. He plucked off some blackberries, plopped them into his mouth, and tossed one to Gunner. "Tastes like June."

As the threat of rain moved in and they were moving downhill, he thought they would be catching a river or stream soon where they should set up camp for the night. The earth smelled damp with the promise of rain.

"I need to get some real shoes. My socks will be wet." He wiggled his toes sticking out from his toeless boots. "Well, how about you, Gunner? You need some shoes too?"

He laughed and played with his dog. He threw pinecones and kicked walnuts and rolled Osage oranges down the road. He laughed when his hound ran off to fetch them.

When Avery came upon a river with a flat, mossy bank, he decided to camp there. Barefooted with Gunner beside him, he sat gazing into the cold, rapid water. He was mesmerized by the colorful pebbles on the sandy bottom. He watched the ripples on the water's surface.

"Whee, Gunner! Boy, did you see that? I almost missed him!" He hurried to his knapsack and pulled out an osnaburg shirt. He waded carefully into the water. He held the shirt by the sleeves letting it drift slowly into the current. Gunner moved to the embankment and gazed at the floating shirt, his ears on alert. Avery squatted slowly; and as the shirt began to spread out between his legs, he spoke quietly to Gunner.

"You ready? Steady. Okay. Now!" Gunner dove into the water, and the beautiful brook trout swam into the shirt. Avery swooped it up in his shirt net and let out a whoop.

"We got him, Gunner, we got him!" They scrambled up the bank, and the fish flip-flopped around on the moss. Gunner laid a paw on the fish, pinning it to the moss.

"Good boy, Gunner, hold him down. This fellow wants to go back home."

He saw another trout surface, snapping a mayfly. The

young fisherman was tempted to try for another. He watched the trout continue downstream, awed by its beauty. Fish and hunt only for food and take only what you need, his father had taught him all his life. Never take living things for sport.

"Waste nothing" was how he was raised. Gunner appreciated that philosophy and enjoyed the fish head. Avery ate supper and set up camp for the night.

Walking along the river the next day, Avery had the feeling that it was going to rain, and perhaps, somewhere, it was already raining. He could smell the rain. Gunner sniffed the air without pausing to evaluate what he was sniffing.

"It's just the rain, Gunner. We need to go deeper into the woods to make camp. It'll keep us a bit drier when the rain comes."

Avery calculated the daylight left and headed into the woods. Before going very far off the trail, Avery was stopped by the awful smell of a dead animal.

"Phewy. Is this what you were sniffing in the air? Boy, I don't think we want to camp here; let's keep going." Gunner ran off investigating, and before long he came back to the trail, dragging a dead rabbit.

"Oh, Gunner, pew, that stinks; where'd you find that?" Gunner dropped it and ran off. He was back shortly, running to catch up with Avery and dragging another rabbit. Dropping the rabbit, he took off again and brought back a bloated woodchuck. Avery kept walking on, and by now he covered his nose, the stench was so bad. Gunner had a string of dead animals lining the trail. Avery walked faster.

"What are all these dead creatures doing here, Gunner?" The smell was making him gag. Gunner continued his search and brought more and more dead animals to present to Avery along the trail. Avery was feeling concerned now, wondering how all these animals had died.

"Gunner, where are all these coming from? No, Gunner, no more. Leave 'em. Something isn't right here. Is the water poisoned?"

He needed to be careful; he tried to reason this out. "They aren't the prey of a raptor or large animal. Any predator would take only what it needed for food, and he'd have eaten it all, wasting nothing." He decided to take a look at one of the animals. Holding his breath, he laid out one of the rabbits with his foot. The rabbit had been shot.

"So it's a human predator."

He hadn't expected that. If a hunter killed a rabbit, he'd dress it for eating and keep its pelt. Why would someone kill it and leave it? This didn't make any sense to Avery. "Without a dog, they might have trouble finding a rabbit they wounded. But *all* of these? No, this doesn't make sense. This is just greed and senseless destruction. Boy, I'd like to get my hands on the person who did this, Gunner. Come on, let's get away from here."

By the time they were far enough away from the stench to set up camp, darkness was descending. Avery moved quickly to get their camp set up. Once they settled in and still got an occasional whiff of the dead animals wafting on a breeze, Avery got angrier and angrier thinking about the carnage. He felt the anger in the pit of his stomach.

Gunner sat up and whined. He walked around pacing. Avery sat up and watched him. Something is out there. Avery could tell by Gunner's behavior. He quietly reached for his musket. He began to hear noises. He heard laughter. *Laughter? In the woods? At night?* Gunner growled low, and Avery picked up his gun and waited. He saw a lantern swinging dangerously. In the ring of light, he caught the faces of two children. Between them, they had a musket that was taller than either of them. They had gone from laughter to arguing and were fighting over the gun.

"Ah gets ta shoot 'er this time," one shouted.

"No, you don't neither, on count ya don't even know how to, an cuz ah em jes bigger'n you, so shut up yer trap; yer sceerin' all them critters, an we won't be shootin us nery thing."

Avery watched them fighting over the musket, which he hoped wasn't ready to fire; and he saw the lantern swinging wildly between them, ready to set fire to something, or someone. *They're small boys; where did they come from? Where's Gunner? What's he doing?* Avery felt panic as he realized these careless little hunters might shoot his dog.

Barking cracked the night air in the woods. The two boys stopped in their tracks. Avery watched them from behind a tree.

"Ah heerd us a wolf," said the bigger one. Gunner continued to bark loudly from his hiding place.

"Ah din't. Ah heerd a dawg. We could use one o' them huntin' dawgs. Maybe we could sell it."

"Well, then how you reckon to git that there dawg, who probly only gon' bite yer leg off?"

"Ah don' know. Ah's tired anyhow."

"Yer a baby. Sit down on yer bee-hind an shut up. I got to do us some huntin'."

Avery watched for the boy to be distracted, then he stepped out onto the trail.

"You boys lost?" he asked.

"Hey!" shouted the surprised bigger boy. But by the time he swung his long musket around, Avery had his hand on it, aiming it toward the ground.

"Git yer hans off'n mah gun!" the little boy shouted. He was struggling, but Avery's one hand was stronger than the little boy's two hands together.

"You need to keep that gun pointed downwards," instructed Avery trying not to sound as angry as he was. "You could accidentally shoot something."

"Yeah, like you, an' it weren't gon be no accident neither." Avery got tired of the struggle and simply yanked the gun away from the boy, who began to pound on Avery. Gunner immediately showed up from his watch and inserted himself into the fracas, barking in the faces of the terrified duo, who without their gun didn't feel quite so brave.

"Let's talk about this hunting trip I hear you're on."

"Who're you anyhow?" the smaller boy asked.

"Maybe I'm the state marshall," smirked Avery, narrowing his eyes. "This is my deputy," he said, pointing to Gunner.

"Who are you?"

"Ain't tellin'," the bigger boy pouted.

"Then I might have to arrest you."

"We din't do nothin'; you cain't 'rest us."

"I believe you did do something. Did you kill all these animals that are lying around?"

"Yeah, ain't no law 'bout that. They's jus critters an we's jus doin target practicin'. We's gittin good too. We's gonna' shoot us sumpin' real big."

"So you can leave it to rot? You aren't hunters; you're just murderers," he said derisively.

Avery wanted to skin these rascals alive. *They're children*, part of him said. *They're murderers*, the other part of him answered. He was struggling to keep his temper under control.

"Aren't you just a little bit sorry for killing all these animals that you didn't need either for food or skins? You just killed them for target practice?" He was steaming, and it was starting to show. The boys were backing down as he came closer and closer to them, towering over them.

"You think they haven't a right to live until they're called to be food? Don't you understand how selfish this is of you? Didn't anyone show you how to take care of an animal that you killed? You don't just leave them lying around. You don't throw them into the water or leave them on the trail with maggots and flies. What's the matter with you?" By now he was shouting; the boys were cowering.

"Well, shoot, we're jes young 'uns," the bigger boy parried.

"Then you're too young for this," Avery said lifting their musket in the air. "This is for responsible, careful, right-thinking people. And that is not you." He knew as he said it that it wasn't their fault. *Where's their father? Who's teaching them?*

"I'm so mad, you're lucky I don't turn this gun on you and shoot you. But I don't do that, your good luck."

"How 'cum you don't do that?" the youngest asked.

"Because it's *wrong*," said Avery, incredulous at the question. "Look, if you need a squirrel or a rabbit for your supper, you come out and get one. You skin it, dress it, cook it, and eat it. Smoke some for tomorrow if you want. If it's winter, you can keep it a day or two. But you only take what you need. It's wrong to take life for any other reason."

"Who cares?" the oldest one asked smartly.

"When you're hungry and there's no game left, it'll be you who cares. But until that time, *I* care. And you'd better care before you get yourself into trouble." Avery was afraid he was the one who was about to get into trouble. His temper was about to take over his good sense.

"What you gonna' do about it," the boy taunted him.

"I'll put you in jail," Avery hissed. The boys backed off a bit, and Gunner growled for effect. "My deputy will take you there. Tomorrow morning I want to see you out here with a shovel. You bury everything you killed. And you set up targets for target practice; and if I ever see you killing critters just for the fun of it, my deputy will take a bite out of you, and I'll put you in jail—or worse!" he shouted. He glared at them and let that sink in.

"Hey, mister, they stink. I don't wanna touch 'em," the bigger boy whined.

"And whose fault is that? You made the mess; you clean it up. Or you can go with my deputy to jail. Your gun will be here when you return in the morning. If you don't come, it's going with me. Go home and go to bed." The boys stared at him but didn't move until Gunner barked. The two jumped and ran back into the woods in the dark with no lantern.

"Aahh, I'm so angry, Gunner. I feel like I'm going to bite my tongue off, I am so mad. Look at those poor animals. Just killing for target practice? Where'd those two get such an idea? Where do they live? In a cave? What kind of heartless little people are they? I want to break them in pieces."

Gunner cocked his head and whined.

Avery stared back. "Yeah, I know. I'm sorry. You make a good deputy. Let's go upwind from the smell and go to bed. I actually didn't do too badly, Gunner, do you think? I mean, I think I did pretty good. Reason and words . . . yeah, I think Father would think that was a pretty good effort."

Gunner made a peculiar, throaty noise and rolled his eyes at Avery.

"Well, what does that mean? Let's go to bed. Hope the breeze doesn't come up stronger or change direction. I feel pretty proud of myself, Gunner—justifiably angry, reason and words. How about that? Maybe I'm catching on."

Before they broke camp in the early morning drizzle, they saw two sniveling little boys digging a hole. A burly man stood behind them with his arms folded across his chest. He had a long scruffy beard, and his hat hung so low Avery couldn't tell how old he was. He said nothing, but he watched the boys digging the hole, and occasionally he spat his chew juice between his boots. When Avery was packed up, he carried their musket and lantern over to the man and handed them to him. The man took the gun in one hand and tipped his hat with the other. He said nothing, just nodded, and Avery turned and walked out of the smelly forest.

Out of the woods and away from the trail, he inhaled deeply and took pleasure in his victory over the battle within. *Yeah, I think Father would've been pleased,* he thought to himself. *It's okay to be justifiably angry, and I didn't punch their nasty runny noses either.*

CHAPTER SIX

BATTLE OF PHILIPPI BRIDGE

They walked all that day in a mist along the turnpike near the winding river, waiting for the rain that was hovering. When he came upon a river with a covered bridge, he decided to take advantage of the shelter the bridge could provide. They made their camp on the bank just under the bridge. It was a pleasant campsite, and Avery was glad they'd stopped early with some daylight still left. He made a fire and began to prepare their supper.

Gunner whined. He pricked up his ears; he pranced. Avery knew his dog was on alert. But what was it he'd heard or smelled or sensed? Avery put out the fire, picked up his gear and musket, and moved down the bank under the trusses of the bridge. He and Gunner hunkered down in the tall reeds and grasses to wait and see what would happen.

Suddenly a sharp crack on the water startled them and caused the tense boy and dog to jump, sprawling all over each other. Picking himself up and looking out to the water, Avery saw two beavers floating toward the current.

"Whew!" breathed Avery. But Gunner wasn't satisfied. He put his paw on Avery's leg and whined.

"What is it, boy? There's something else, isn't there. Okay. We'll stay here."

His answer came with boisterous voices of a small company of soldiers coming toward the bridge across the Tygart River.

They started to set up their camp. Avery peered at them through the trusses.

"Who are they, Gunner? They aren't organized enough to be an army." More were coming down the road, a bit helter-skelter, he thought. He watched them noisily and carelessly spreading out their camp site. Maybe they were the Home Guard. But, no, the Home Guard was made up of small groups of secretive men. Maybe they were marauders? No, this was too large a group for marauders, who tended to run in small gangs. Maybe they were deserters. They could be deserters, he calculated. Deserters from both sides hung together for safety. And he knew they wouldn't like to be seen.

"We'll stay here till it's dark," he whispered, "just in case."

Gunner seemed to be in agreement and lay quietly at Avery's feet.

He could hear them talking, gaming, and making jokes about the Union army. He figured out that they were a company of Confederate soldiers, mostly new on the job, when he heard their plans to take this bridge and the nearby railroad in the morning. They were planning with great bravado.

"This might be the war, Gunner."

After dark, Avery and Gunner wrapped up in their blanket and bedded down under the bridge. They slept to the sound of soft rain on the bridge.

At daybreak Gunner began to pace. Avery looked across the river through the trestles. It had rained during the night. Huge spider webs spun in beautiful geometric designs, glistening with rain drops like a sparkling necklace, delicate and out of place, hung under the bridge. Beyond the spider webs, the soldiers were moving around casually. Avery smelled their chicory coffee. But Gunner wasn't looking across the water. His eyes were focused on the surrounding hills. Avery squinted into the morning light. Across the tops of the hills in black silhouette, there was movement, a lot of movement, once his eyes adjusted. *It looks like a march of carpenter ants on a trail in an old pine stand*, he observed, *thousands of carpenter ants. But these aren't ants. They are soldiers.*

"I think we might need a new place to be, Gunner. But how'll we do that and not be seen?"

The encampment was getting louder. He heard the banging and scraping of mess tins. He gathered his gear and crawled back up the bank, staying low in the safety of the trees. He watched the soldiers; he and Gunner crawled parallel with the road, staying in the trees.

"How'll we ever get across?" The soldiers were all standing in the mess line facing away from Avery, banging their bowls and insulting their cook. Avery saw their chance.

"Okay, Gunner, move." The two of them crossed the road quickly and took cover in a thicket of dog hobble on the other side. "Don't worry, Gunner. If I have to carry you out, I will. We won't let this dog hobble hobble you."

Before too long, they felt a slight tremor beneath them. The heavy caissons and cannon were rolling. The ground trembled. Gunner's ears were up.

"It feels like we might be about to see something, Gunner. Could be the war." He was aware of movement and shadows on the far side of the road and upward toward the hills. Instinctively, he knew the soldiers were on the move toward the bridge. The army on the other side was in various stages of disarray. When the bugle charge sounded, what looked to Avery like thousands of soldiers came off the hillsides, out of the trees, and down the road.

The little encampment at the bridge was caught completely by surprise. Vastly outnumbered with no sentries posted and most men and officers unarmed and unprepared for such an encounter, their commanding officer had no choice but to order a hasty retreat. The Confederate soldiers ran pell-mell in disgrace.

The Union soldiers captured the bridge and also a large quantity of supplies and munitions that were left behind. No shots were fired.

Avery and Gunner peered through the thicket of dog hobble and watched the soldiers carry off their booty.

"Well, Gunner, I think we just saw the war," he said to his panting dog. "That wasn't so bad."

Avery pulled his oilcloth tightly over his pack as the sky darkened. The rain had moved in, and it didn't stop. Everything Avery owned was wet. His tarpaulin sagged with water and his rubber sheet had as many holes as a cider press. The pages of his little Bible were stuck together. The mountain roads were a quagmire. Many streams and creeks were impassable. Avery had lost all track of time. How long had it been raining? How many days had they sloshed along in the mud and water? He broke camp mechanically. He was cold, wet, and miserable. His dog was caked in mud.

"So this is why the eastern folks call this the wilderness," he mumbled glumly and began to climb upward.

He slid backwards and pulled himself forward by grabbing vines and saplings; two pulls upward, one slide backwards. Gunner bounded, slid, bounded, slid, and found himself soaking wet and covered with mud on the summit of Laurel Mountain, ahead of Avery. The two of them stood on the summit of the knob together looking down at the broad expanse of Tygart Valley. Much of the valley was under water, and the rain continued. He took out his compass, took his bearing, and decided the Staunton-Parkersburg Turnpike should be right over there; he pointed it out to Gunner.

Sliding down the slippery, muddy, hillside was treacherous and exhausting. Pausing under a cluster of trees to catch his breath, Avery slid his heavy gear to the ground and leaned against the tree. He hardly noticed the steady rain pelting his face, he was so tired. Avery didn't remember ever seeing it rain this many consecutive days in his life. Gunner lay down beside him. Avery didn't know he'd dozed off until he was awakened by Gunner's excited barks and bellows.

Gunner bounded and danced in a wide circle increasing in distance away from Avery. Eyes wide open and Gunner at a far enough distance, Avery was able to see that what the dog was circling was a knot of two rattlesnakes coiled together. The gray timber rattlers were shaking their angry castanets and striking out at Gunner from two directions. The clever dog stayed on the outside of their circle, giving him the advantage and moving the snakes away from Avery.

Avery's mind was moving rapidly. What did he have? What could he use? How could he not endanger Gunner and still get the snakes away? Avery knew that the timber rattler carried enough venom to kill a man even with a small bite. He grabbed his heavy knapsack and approached the knotted, coiled snakes.

"Gunner, off!" He heaved the heavy knapsack, as forcefully as he could, onto the snakes. He knew the snakes would be angry when they recovered, and Gunner needed to be out of their way. He thought the knapsack would only stun them momentarily, and he was right. The knapsack flipped and flopped, and gradually one angry head with gleaming eyes slithered out toward the dog.

"Gunner, come!" Gunner abruptly changed directions and came to Avery, leaving the snake to glide angrily off into the woods. The second snake rattled loudly under the knapsack. Avery reached for his musket. He turned it upside down to use the heavy stock for a club, if the snake should head his way.

The timber rattler was a beautiful snake with intricate embroidery that Avery had always admired from a distance. He didn't want to kill it, but if it was necessary to protect Gunner or himself, then he needed to be ready.

The knapsack was moving across the wet ground slowly tipping first to one side, then the other. Avery thought it looked more like a harmless tortoise moving than a snake, but he was waiting and ready if the snake decided to come out and strike. Gunner followed the moving knapsack with interest.

"Gunner, back off!" The snake was coiled under the knapsack and Avery knew it could strike out on any side. Still the knapsack slid slowly across the mud, tottering back and forth. When it lodged against a large tree root and could go no further, the snake, continuing its forward motion, slid under the tree root and disappeared into the ground. The rattles quieted as the snake uncoiled. It seemed to have disappeared into the hollow under the tree.

Avery sighed a big relief and, still shaking, reached for the knapsack. In that instant Gunner flew after the knapsack, and in the blink of an eye he whipped the snake against the tree, breaking the snake's back. The limp snake dangled from Gunner's mouth like a piece of rope. Avery stood stunned taking it all in.

"What just happened?"

When his mind began to work again, he realized that his dog had just saved his life.

"Drop it, Gunner," he commanded weakly. The dog dropped the dead snake. "Well done." He hugged his dog. "Thank you, boy; I don't know how you knew, but . . . thank you."

He dropped to his shaking knees and thanked God for his safety and for his dog. He admired the snake, but he didn't pick it up; even a dead snake could still bite. Still shaken, Avery and Gunner moved on in the steady rain.

"Gunner, were you scared, boy? I sure was. I didn't know it then, but I sure know it now. Do you think that makes me a baby? I'm trying to be grown up about it, but I was really scared. My knees are still wobbly." His companion licked his hand reassuringly as they sloshed along in the rain and the mud.

CHAPTER SEVEN

A FRIEND IN THE WILDERNESS

They slogged along in the rain through the summer days and nights. He wondered if it would rain forever. The turnpike took them across another wet, fertile valley.

"There must be a farm somewhere, Gunner. Someone must husband this land. There must be somebody around who might have seen Uncle Fredric." And before long, in the steadily falling rain and gray, low-lying fog, Avery made out the silhouettes of farm buildings. He imagined hot corn bread and herb tea, maybe some potatoes or beets, maybe apple pie, and maybe they'd be invited in. Jowls slobbering, Gunner looked up at him, as if he could read Avery's thoughts.

The farm looked like it was once a substantial holding, but now it seemed to be abandoned. Perhaps they could just go in, have a fire, a roof overhead, and be out of the rain. He walked around the unkempt yard. It looked to Avery like someone was either very lazy or the farm had been abandoned for some time. His father often quoted a verse from Ecclesiastes 10 which meant that if a man is lazy, the rafters sag; and if his hands are idle, the roof leaks. He could see evidence of that truth here. He could see a good-sized barn, a tool shed, a privy, a potting barn, and the house, all in stages of deterioration. He could see abandoned corrals and pens, an empty pig sty, and a smokehouse that was collapsing.

"Where did they all go? Probably it's the war," he decided

with a sigh. He went up on the porch, where it seemed good to be out of the rain.

Just then the door flew open on a pair of lopsided, rusty hinges, and in the doorway stood the funniest looking old woman Avery had ever seen. He wanted to laugh, but it wouldn't be polite; and she seemed so fierce, he decided it wouldn't be wise.

She was a curious looking woman, smaller than his mother, shorter than he. Her hair was frizzled and stuck out all over her head in little knots like barbed wire. Her clothes were filthy, and it was obvious by the smell that she hadn't taken them off in quite a while. Her purplish brown face and neck were scarred, and her eyes were squinted and matted. She was wielding a broom, which she swung back and forth wildly, like she was angrily sweeping cobwebs from the air.

"I don' know who you uns are, but yer best git off'n my porch. I don' be lookin' fer no troubles, but I ken kill yer fer bein' here as this here's my land, and yer best be gitten off it raht now!" Her voice cracked as it reached the crescendo.

"I'm sorry, ma'am," said Avery, ducking the sweeping broom. "We didn't mean to scare you. My name is Avery Junior Bennett, and this is my dog, Gunner. We don't mean you any harm. We only need some shelter from the rain, and we'll be happy to work for it. We won't cause you any trouble. I can cut wood and do things for you." He studied the empty wood box. "I know how to do about everything on a farm, and I'm a good worker. We'd just like to get out of the rain for a while. Please?"

"Yer jest a boy?"

"Well, ma'am, I'm fourteen years, not too small a boy."

She lowered the broom. "Yer lookin' to steal my things? If yar', yer too late. It's done been stoled a'ready. They's nothin' left here."

"Oh, no, ma'am. I won't take anything, I promise. I'm a peaceable person, and I don't covet nor steal." Avery watched her face contorting in thought and realized the woman couldn't see him.

"Okay then, you and yer dog come on inside."

Inside, Avery looked around and saw that he might have been too quick to volunteer. The inside of the house smelled like a chamber pot forgotten, only worse. The fire had gone out long ago, and the coals were cold, damp, and musty smelling. He saw no signs of living at all. The table was missing two legs and stood up on end. Chair parts were scattered, and only one chair was still put together. Pots and dusty dishes were lying about, the cabinets opened, and the shelves empty.

The woman scratched herself mightily and stumbled around the littered floor to the corner, where her dirty cot and heaps of tattered, filthy blankets lay in a pile, still warm from her body. She dropped to the cot and lay looking up at the ceiling.

"Do you live here alone?" asked Avery.

"Why you want to know?" she snarled. "You figure to take advantage of me?"

"Oh no, not at all. Just . . . just interested is all."

"I'm alone," she snapped. "Not how it should be, but how it is."

"When did you eat last?"

"Don' know and don' care."

"Aren't you hungry?" He sure was hungry.

"Cain't be bothered t' think on it."

Avery looked around. He sat down on the stone hearth, there not being anywhere else to sit except the one chair, which he didn't trust.

"Well," he said in his friendliest tone, "what's your name?"

"Who's a' askin'?"

"Well, just me, ma'am. I'm Avery Junior Bennett, and this is Gunner, my dog."

"Ya said that a' ready," she snapped.

"Yes, ma'am, I did. It's just manners. I just wanted to make your acquaintance."

"Why?"

"I thought we might like to know what to call one another, if I was going to do some work for you, and you'd let me stay a while. I'd like to call you by your name, like . . . Mrs. Some-body, you know."

"Ha, ha, ha," she cackled and slapped her stomach. "That's a good one. Mrs. Somebody," she laughed.

Avery felt his face flush.

"Yeah," she said, "that's me, ol' Mrs. Somebody, the lady of the house."

"Should I call you that? Mrs. Somebody?" He felt embar-rassed.

"I reckon that's as good a name as ever I had, ha, ha. Mrs. Somebody. How 'bout that?"

"Well, then, I'll see what I can get doing here for you," he said, in a hurry to escape this conversation. He looked around the house again. Mrs. Somebody began to snore.

Avery and Gunner went back outside to take a quick in-ventory. In the barn he found the winter's store of hay in the loft for horses, who were absent from their stalls. The other side of the barn had three milking stalls, where three little stools sat idly next to the empty milk pails, but no cows.

The privy full of webs and animal filth, where he needed to make a stop, had obviously not been in use for a while. He pushed the door in and disturbed the sleeping bats that protested and dropped off the wall.

The pump had rusted; it squeaked and groaned when he pumped the handle, begging to be primed. He decided to do this job first, so he could wash his hands. *After a trip to this privy, it would be necessary*, he thought.

The garden shed was full of rusted tools. The webs, the mold, and the dead mice all told the story of abandonment. Stand-ing in the rain surveying the puddles, Avery found it hard to know the whereabouts or the sizes of any gardens. From the tool shed he selected a saw, a can of lubricant, and a honing stone, and he returned to the house. On the cold, damp porch, Avery began to clean the rust off the saw, lubricate, and sharpen it. When he was satisfied that it would be an effective tool, he ran back to the barn. He gathered up two of the little milking stools and sawed the legs off. Putting the dry wooden pieces in a feed sack to keep them dry, he carried them back to the house.

Mrs. Somebody was still snoring. Avery cleared away the damp charcoal and ashes from the fireplace; he swept away the webs. He reached up the chimney as far as he could reach with her broom and swept, beat, and spun the broom around. A flutter of wings and startled chirps broke the silence of the room. Nesting materials dropped down on him. Gunner looked up the chimney and whined wistfully. When Avery was satisfied with his fireplace, he put a little of the lubricant on one of the sawed legs, crumbled up some newsprint that had fallen out of the chinking in the wall, and laid the stool legs in the fireplace. He hoped he still had some dry sulfur matches left in his knapsack.

"Lighter's in the Mason jar in the cupboard," growled a hoarse, raspy voice from the cot. Avery was startled. Processing the words, he began to look in the cupboards. There was the green glass Mason jar. He unscrewed the tin lid and found the dry matches. In a bigger jar next to the matches, he found some little fat kindling pieces. Hopeful, Avery struck a match and touched it to the fat kindling. It snapped, sputtered, and began to burn. Carefully he placed it under the little tent of chair legs and other pieces of dry wood from the shed. A stream of smoke began to rise up the chimney; the fire was burning and crackling. But he knew it would take steady feeding to keep the fire going. Suddenly he understood what had happened to the table legs and the missing pieces of furniture.

He swept the hearth and all around the fireplace with the old woman's broom and stacked a wood pile in the wood box next to the chimney, using the rest of the table legs and chair parts.

He'd put the milk pails in the yard to collect rain water to pour into the pump to prime it. It screeched into use; Avery put a drop of lubricant into the ball joint. Before long, a rusty colored stream of water gushed from the pump. He kept pumping until he thought his arms would fall off. Gradually the water began to clear. He collected a bucketful of clean water, took it in to the fire, hung the pail on the hearth crane, and heated the water.

A faded cloth, which appeared to be a tablecloth, lay discarded in the corner on the floor. Avery figured when the legs came off the table, the cloth just slid off onto the floor and was never picked up. He picked it up, shook out the dust, and tore it into smaller squares. When the water was warm he used the cloth squares to wash the dusty pans and dishes and wiped out the cupboards. His mother had taught him the proverb "Cleanliness is next to godliness," so he cleaned the cupboard and put the mostly clean dishes on the cleaner shelves.

He swept the partly plank, partly dirt floor. He refilled the pail with clean water, hung it back on the crane, fed the fire, and went out to the tool shed. He walked around the muddy yard, stamping and prodding the ground with the handle of a hoe. He was sure it would be here under the mud and accumulated soil. Gunner hadn't wanted to leave the fire, but he reluctantly joined Avery in the rain. Gunner watched Avery drag the hoe, beat the handle, and prod the soil.

"I'm sure it's around here, Gunner. Most farms would have it near the house, near the tools, and away from the privy and pig wallow. Yep. I think it's going to be about here."

The helpful dog began walking circles around Avery, nose down, paws prancing his little tracking dance. Before long, about ten yards beyond where Avery stood, Gunner began to dig.

"You got something, Gunner? Good boy!"

Avery jabbed the hoe handle where Gunner dug and heard the wood reverberate with a hollow *thunk*.

"You got it, Gunner. Thank you, good dog."

Uncovering the wooden door buried in mud and disuse, he lifted it and peered down into the darkness.

"Thanks, Gunner. You found the old root cellar, all right. Hope it's got something in it."

He lowered himself down three steps into the darkness. The smell of the damp, dirt floor, gunny bags, and pungent green walnuts was a nostalgic reminder of home. He climbed back out and went into the house to get his lantern. With the small light from his lantern, he found what he was looking for. Some of the roots had dried or rotted; he noted they hadn't been as carefully stored as his mother would've done. But there were a few potatoes, some yams, and a sack of walnuts. There were beets, a crock of sauerkraut, a heap of turnips stored in straw, and a crock of pickles. There were a few wrinkled apples. Avery selected a few items and hauled them up the stairs, lowered the door, and went back in the house.

He cleared away dust and clutter in segments to give himself a place to work. He wiped off the table that was now laying flat on the floor with no legs and went to work with his Bowie knife. He soon had a watery broth simmering on the hook over the fire.

"Mrs. Somebody," Avery said quietly. "Mrs.Somebody?"

She jerked into a sitting position and began swinging her arms. "Leave me be," she shouted. "Leave me."

"I didn't mean to scare you, ma'am. I just wanted to wake you to have a bit of supper."

"Oh, it's yer again." She stopped waving her arms. "Supper? What ya talkin' 'bout supper? You s'posin to have a mean joke on this ol' body? Supper, hmpf."

"No ma'am. I cooked us up a little supper. Sit this way," he said, and he moved her legs over the edge of the cot. She weighed less than a bucket of milk, Avery thought. He washed her fingers with a warm wet cloth and his soap.

"Now then, you just wait here a minute, and I'll bring you a little supper."

He put a cup of broth and vegetables on an iron griddle that worked well as a tray. A cup of hot herbal tea and a piece of hardtack from his knapsack all sat on the griddle tray across the old woman's bony knees.

He picked her hand up gently and lightly touched everything with her fingers.

"It's hot, but there it all is so you can find it." She said nothing, but held the griddle with one hand and fumbled around with the other. She sipped her broth and tea, and she ate the hardtack with hungry lust. A tear slipped out from the closed eyelid and left a trace down her dirty face.

"How you know to cook, Mr. Fourteen-Years-Old Avery Junior Bennett?"

Avery smiled; she remembered his name. *That's a good beginning*, he thought.

"My mother showed me. She says everyone needs to know how to look after himself." Avery asked the blessing, and they ate in friendly silence.

When she'd finished eating, she mopped her broth with the hardtack.

"I cain't see. I ain't got no eyes."

"What happened to your eyes?"

"They got blowed plumb out my skull, that's what happen. Them blamed Home Guard, they call theyselves. Guard of the devils is what they be. They come here lookin' for my menfolk. Says they got to come do they duty. I say, I ain't got no menfolk, and they say I's lyin'. Says I got to support the war effort, and since I says they ain't no men, they just take everthing I do have. They took my winter surplus, my stock, my garden, my staples, and my everthin'.

"I throwed my lantern at 'em. They throwed it back, and it 'sploded in my face, an caught my hair on fire, an' blew my eyes nigh out my head. My face got all blistered up, and I cain't see night fer day. Don't even know how long ago that would be. But I's just bidin' my time here waitin' and wantin' to be starved to death or froze and get taken to the great yonder. Yes, sir, boy, when that chariot comes, I be ready!"

Avery came close to her and took her tray. She smelled bad, but he wanted to see her eyes up close. He could see now that the scars were from burns. Her frizzled funny hair had been burned. But the eyes . . . he could see the eyelids puffed out over the orb of the eyeball. Jack the blacksmith, who came to their farm to shoe their horses, had only one eye, and the lid that covered the missing eye was sunken in. Mrs. Somebody's looked like she might have some big eyes under her scarred lids. Now that he was seeing her up close, he could see that there were no eyelashes or eyebrows. Avery studied her face.

"Mrs. Somebody, I think your eyes might still be there. The lids are covering them."

"Well, if they's in there, they's broke. The 'splosion must have broke 'em cause they cain't see nothin'."

"Do your eyes hurt when you touch them?"

"Don' know. I don' touch 'em. Why you care?"

"Because I think I might be able to help you with your eyes. Maybe your eyes aren't really gone, or even broken; maybe they're just covered up. If they don't hurt when you touch them, would you allow me to try to open them?"

"Shoot! I got me a Mr. Do-Gooder, right here in my own house. Don't matter to me none, Mr. Fourteen-Year-Old Avery Do-Gooder. I'm just as soon die as not, but if it'll make yer feel good, then you jes' make yerself at home." She coughed out a derisive little laugh, tossed herself back on the cot, and looked up at the ceiling, waiting for her chariot.

Avery cooled the boiled water. He sorted through his assortment of herbs and tinctures, salves and poultices, but he didn't see anything that he thought might be useful. *What would Mother chose?* he pondered.

He took out some of his clean bandages and put them in the warm water. He laid them on the woman's eyes, soaking them with warm water and gentleness. After several applications, he began to see some of the crust loosening. He brushed the particles carefully off her face away from her eyes. After several hours of this procedure the old woman looked like a raccoon. The soaks, which had removed the crust, also removed several layers of soot around her eyes. It tickled him; he tried not to laugh. When most of the crust was removed, he asked her if she could open her eyes.

"I told yer, I cain't see. Don' you listen? How kin I open my eyes if I cain't see to open 'em up?"

"Just open them up like it was morning, like you used to do before all this happened."

"Cain't."

Avery touched the top of one lid and pulled upward just a little.

"Ouch!" the old woman screeched. "Yer tryin' ter take off my hide?"

It was all Avery could do to keep from laughing; she was so comical. He repeated the soaks, which she seemed to enjoy, and then he tried again. This time he saw a sliver—just a little crack—of eyeball under one lid. It looked to Avery like the scarring had crossed from lid to cheek, effectively sealing the eye shut with a healing layer of skin. He was disappointed because he'd hoped that removing the crusting would release the eye lid. He gently spread some of his mother's honey salve for softening skin around her eyes and cheeks. She smiled.

"Feels raht nice," she cooed. He covered her with her dirty blankets, banked the fire, and he and Gunner went to the barn to sleep in the hay. He was exhausted.

As daylight seeped into the barn, Avery crept back into the house, stoked the fire, put on some water, and he and Gunner went hunting. They returned with a rabbit and a quail. He dressed them and prepared them for eating. He added the rabbit to the stew, which was simmering from last night. He threaded the quail onto a rusty spit over the fire.

Mrs. Somebody awoke to the pleasant aroma of cooking food. He watched her get up and fumble around for the walls, bumping, grumbling, and stumbling her way to the door. Outside the door, she hiked up her skirts, relieved herself, and stumbled back inside, feeling her way to the cot.

Avery cleared his throat. "Morning Mrs. Somebody."

"Yer watchin' me?" she demanded.

"No ma'am. Not deliberately anyway."

"Nature calls, and one's gotter tend to it. Even animals don't soil in them's beds. I gotter do what I gotter do. That's that."

"Yes, ma'am, I understand, of course." Avery now understood the smell at the door way, and he had a plan.

"Here's some warm water, and this stocking has lye soap in it. You can wash your face and hands; I'll have breakfast ready in a little bit," he promised.

He watched her fumble with the soap and splash the water. Her fingernails were long, curved, and filthy. He thought about the little scissors in his sewing kit. Avery bowed his head and gave thanks; they ate in silence. The old woman lay back down. Avery gathered up the leftovers and fed them to his dog, who'd been waiting patiently for his share of the bounty that he'd helped provide.

In the tool shed and the barn, Avery gathered every rope, string, and fence wire he could find. He hammered garden stakes into the soft, wet ground. He hammered them in straight lines from the door to the privy. He strung the ropes, strings, leather bridle straps, or fence wire around each of the stakes. By afternoon he was leading the old woman, in the rain, out the door.

"Reach here," he instructed her and placed her hand on the rope. "Now, walk, but don't let go of the rope," he said. She stumbled along with the assortment of ropes passing through her fist. She ran smack into the privy door.

"This a joke? You makin' fun o' me?" she fumed.

"No ma'am. You've just come all on your own to the privy. Now you can answer nature's call all the better. Here is the door hole; pull it out. Now step up one step, turn around, and there you are!" he announced proudly.

"Hmpf," she snorted. "Perty good." He showed her how to take herself back to the house. Wearing Avery's rubber sheet draped over her, she practiced the route several times that day in the rain, just to get the hang of it.

Avery spread straw around the doorway to give them a drier and pleasanter entrance. Another day he'd make more rope paths so she could learn to walk to the barn, get things from the root cellar, and find the tools, which he had laid out orderly in the tool shed. If it ever stopped raining, she'd be able to get out more, he thought. This rain was making all three of them sour, he groused.

Inside, Avery stoked the fire. Gunner lay down next to the fire with his chin on his paws and watched Avery as he strung a rope clothesline across the room. He draped his rubber sheet and tarpaulin over the line to dry out and hung his shirt and under-clothes next to the fire. His knapsack was so wet, he wondered if it would ever dry out before mildew covered it. He fixed them some turnips for supper; they ate the quail and shelled some walnuts. He soaked her hands in a pail of soapy water and trimmed her fingernails. He told her to wash herself and her clothes and hang the clothes on the line to dry over night.

"I got some other clothes," she announced unexpectedly. "They'd be in the clothes press over there by the cabinet. Yer see a clothes press?"

Avery looked at the pile of splintered furniture he'd stacked in the firebox.

"No, ma'am, I don't." Avery sadly shook his head. "You get your bath now, and I'll see you in the morning." He banked the fire and went out to the barn where he hung his own wet clothes on the stall doors, on bridle hooks, and lantern nails. He rolled up in his damp blanket and dug himself a little cave in the hay. Gunner curled up next to him, and they warmed each other, while they listened to the relentless rain beating a rhythm on the barn roof.

"What kind of person would do such a thing, Gunner? Who would take everything from an old woman?" He felt the old nemesis working its way through his body. Gunner rolled over and let out a deep sigh with all four legs in the air. Avery looked at his fist and took a deep breath, exhaling his outrage, and releasing his fist.

"Yeah, I'm tired too." He matched Gunner's deep sighs. They listened to the rain and fell asleep.

In the morning, he went quietly into the house and stoked the fire. He was relieved to see that the woman's clothes were hanging on the clothesline. He hoped she'd smell a bit fresher today. He warmed some water and tossed in some vegetables. She stirred under the covers, and Avery, not wanting to surprise or embarrass her again, spoke up.

"Good morning, Mrs. Somebody. I'm in here now, but I'm going out to do some chores. You can get dressed, and I'll be back in shortly. That okay?"

"I see you," she said softly.

"What did you say?" He moved to her cot. "You can see me?"

"I said that, Mr. Avery Junior Bennett. You got a tater in yer ear? I said I can see you." Now she sounded like her old self, but she was smiling.

"What can you see?" he asked eagerly.

"I c'n see a little peep hole o' light. Jes' a little bitty peep hole, an' you are in it. I think it's day."

"Yes, yes, that's right. It is day. It's just like I thought, Mrs. Somebody. We must keep soaking them every day."

"Ma' eyes ain't blowed out my head," she said in disbelief. "I thought they was. And they ain't even broke. I thought they was." She sounded like an amazed child.

"I'm going out now, so you get up and get dressed so we can eat." Avery thought he sounded more and more like a grownup, or a parent. He missed his parents.

Day after day the rain came down. Avery cut wood, pumped water, chopped a vegetable, went hunting, and dried their clothes by the fire. When he and Gunner got lucky, he dressed meat, smoked it, salted it, stewed it, and ate some for supper.

He moved things around to make it easier for the old woman to get around the house. She spent less time on her cot these days, he noticed. He brought in some stumps for sitting. He washed her hair and read to her from his Bible. He was surprised to learn that she knew many Psalms by heart, though she'd never learned to read.

"I never got the hang of memorizing scripture verse," Avery confessed to her. "I admire you that you can do it so well. You're pretty smart, Mrs. Somebody."

"Ya think that, do ya?" Avery could tell that the compliment pleased her.

One morning while he was pumping water, something wonderful happened. The rain stopped, and the sun came out. Avery was beginning to believe that it would rain forever. In a couple of days, the ground began to dry out. He brought tools out of the tool shed. He searched the barn, the potting shed, and the root cellar for any seed, root, or tuber that looked like it might be alive enough to grow.

He'd carefully shaken any loose seeds from the dried herbs, which were hanging from the kitchen rafters. Avery had set shallow pans of water in front of the kitchen window where he'd placed potato eyes, tips of yams, the ends of some turnips, beet root, and a wasted carrot. He'd saved these from the meals he'd prepared for Mrs. Somebody. Now they were all sprouting. He said a prayer of thanks and gathered them up.

He gently pushed them under the surface of the rich loam in rows. He found grains of corn from a gnawed gunny bag that the mice had missed. He didn't have much hope for them, but what did he have to lose? He'd soak them and plant them too.

In the potting shed, he'd noticed a shelf stacked with Mason jars that were filled with seeds. He recognized pumpkin seeds, or maybe they were squash; there were watermelon seeds, and some morning glory seeds, peas, and beans. He didn't know what else or whether they were edible, but he planted one half of everything he found. Then he prayed. The farm boy knew all these things should've been planted in the spring. Now it was summer; would they have enough time to grow before the winter? He prayed harder.

The weather continued to improve with brilliant warm days and a drying breeze. Avery washed all the bed covers and laid them over bushes to dry. He took a good look at the branches of the bushes and decided they were figs. He noticed new green shoots in straight lines in the garden. Perhaps Mrs. Somebody wouldn't starve to death after all. He and Gunner brought home a squirrel and a grouse to prepare for her.

At supper that night, he said, "Mrs. Somebody, there's something I need to talk to you about tonight."

"Don' ya go chimin' on about sentimentals, Mr. Fourteen-Year-Old Farmer Boy. I know'd ya'd be leavin' when yer showed up. A feller's gotter do what he's gotter do and finish what he was settin' out ter do. So's yer jes be goin' on."

"That's not it, Mrs. Somebody. I mean, there's more." So he told her about the garden and all the other rope walks he'd made for her. He told her it was really important to go all the way out to the privy.

"You have to always wash your hands good before you handle the food, Mrs. Somebody. My mother told me that's really important, so you don't get sick." He showed her how the tools were laid out, so she could get to them.

"They're all cleaned and sharpened," he told her. "The wood box is full. The pump needs to be primed occasionally, but tomorrow I'll show you all of this." She was listening attentively.

"And whenever I can, I'll come back and see how you're getting on. I believe that your eyelids could get all the way un-stuck with a doctor to help you. But all the doctors are busy right now, I think. Gunner and me, well, we won't forget about you. And I'll pray about you. We thank you for your hospitality and your shelter in the rain. We're beholden to you."

"I a'ready tol' yer, no sentimentals, boy-o. It's me what owes that thanks, only I'm not so good at it. I b'lieve yer done saved ma' life, boy."

After supper they washed the dishes together, and Avery gathered all his belongings. He and Gunner went to the pleasant barn for the last time. Across the barren fields they could hear the whippoorwill trilling his lullaby. Gunner sighed and laid his chin on his paws; his eyes slowly closed. Avery laid his head on his arms and fell asleep.

At sun up he stoked the fire, pumped the water, ate a little stewed squirrel, and shared a portion with Gunner. He took Mrs. Somebody all around the farm on her rope walks and helped her learn where to find everything. He packed his damp knap-sack, walked out into the sunshine, and whistled for his dog. They headed once more for the turnpike.

"Hey! Hey you, Mr. Fourteen-Years-Old Avery Junior Bennett from Kanawha!" she called after him in her cracked voice. "Be safe. And it's Rose."

"What's Rose?"

"Me. That's mah name. Rose Holtom. It's been nice to meet 'cha." She turned and walked back into her house.

Avery smiled. "Goodbye, Rose Holtom. Mrs. Somebody, take care of yourself." Gunner pricked up his ears, whipped his tail, and headed off down the lane to the road. "We'll be back sometime, God willing."

CHAPTER EIGHT

NO TIME
FOR A PICNIC

Avery had no real idea what the date was or how long he had tarried. The month-long rain had caused him to lose all track of time. Days were long and hot, so he figured it must be deep into summer. It sure did smell good out in the sunshine! Gunner ran ahead of him chasing invisible prey for the sport of it. Avery had cut the toes out of his boots so long ago that now his growing toes actually hung over the sole. His britches were snug, and a good bit of leg was showing. He noticed that his skinny legs were getting strong, muscular, and hairy. He felt a bit self conscious about that wondering if anyone would notice. But then, who would be around to notice?

The turnpike seemed devoid of local folk and travelers. He occasionally saw columns of soldiers walking in both directions. He heard ambulance wagons carrying groaning and grotesque forms. He watched ragged men painfully dragging along on walking sticks. Sometimes he came upon soldiers burying their dead. Whenever he had the opportunity, he asked about Uncle Fredric. He understood more about the war with each passing day.

Days and nights went by, and except for nighttime dew, it was dry. The sun came up, and the sun set; days got hotter and stickier. Mosquitoes buzzed about his ears and neck. Avery rubbed himself with the salve that his mother made to keep the mosquitoes from biting; she believed mosquito bites caused illness. He often heard artillery off in the distance. One day he heard sounds of battle that lasted all day, and he could see smoke clouds hovering on the horizon, thick and phosphorous.

He was surprised one afternoon to see a large gathering of people moving up a hillside. He could see the activity from the turnpike. On the hilltop against the white hot sky, silhouettes took shape of ladies holding parasols, children running, and knots of men talking. He hadn't seen many civilians on the turnpike for days. These people must be from a holler on the other side of this mountain, he figured. Perhaps, then, there's a town. Maybe there'd be some shoes for a boy who'd be willing to work for them, he hoped. He and Gunner climbed the hill.

At the top, all was festive. People spread out their quilts and unloaded picnic baskets, while their children raced around the hillside. Gunner wagged his tail and went off to make friends with the owners of the picnic baskets.

Avery listened to conversations and introduced himself to a few folks. He smiled at a family eating a picnic spread out on their quilt. The red-haired child reminded him of the taters. He watched and he listened, but he was totally unable to absorb what he was learning about this festive scene.

These townsfolk came to watch an actual battle that would be fought on the field in a glen beneath them on the other side of the hill. They came to watch the cannon and the guns fill the air with smoke and sulfur. They hoped to see men get bloodied, injured, and maybe even die. They wanted to see who'd win, as if it were a Saturday afternoon race at the fairground. Men were taking bets. Laughter and happy excitement filled the air. His stomach churned; he was both confused and angry.

Along his journey on the turnpike, he saw companies returning from skirmishes. He saw infantry men who appeared to be limping in their sleep; he saw wagons piled with bodies, followed by swarms of flies. Didn't any of these people on the hill understand that war was serious? Did they think this was a good game for the children, for spectators, to enjoy? Were they cheering for their favorite contestant? He felt disgusted.

A lady offered him a boiled egg and a slice of melon. He

declined politely and leaned against a tree. He felt his temper rising with each shallow breath.

Gunner looked longingly at the tray of eggs and wandered around the crowd looking polite, friendly, and hopeful. Avery felt nauseated and dropped into a squat with his back against the tree away from the people. He watched Gunner harvesting crumbs, as he followed the children.

"A picnic? A picnic?" He shook his head, disbelieving. He took some deep breaths and unfolded his hands in his lap. He heard orders shouted down below and the rumble of artillery wagons on the move. The partying crowd, quieting in anticipation, all turned and faced down the slope.

"Why don't they shoot?" a man said.

"What're they waiting for?" said another.

"Come on, get it going. We don't have all day," someone urged.

"Let's see what you got!" a man bellowed through his cupped hands.

"Care to wager anyone?"

The crowd was restless and eager for battle. Avery wanted to shout at them and shake them. *Don't you know? War isn't a game.* He bit his lip and pressed his head into his hands. He would not, could not, watch.

The first cannon fired and several of the spectators cheered. A blood-curdling howl from one side was answered by the cannon's blast from the other, and the battle ensued. The crowd roared their approval. With his head in his hands and his back to the tree, Avery faced away from the battlefield below. He didn't need to see it to know what was happening. On the field below men were shot, arms and legs shattered; soldiers and horses died. On the hill the spectators cheered, women fainted, and children played soldier. It didn't last terribly long, but long enough.

Before the sun was set in the west, the spectators, their baskets, their children, and their wagons were gone from the hill. The air was rancid with the smell of gunpowder. Avery finally looked down at the quiet battlefield. Only a few men remained there. They dragged bodies into wagons, put the wounded on litters, and hoisted them into ambulance wagons. Some headed east and the rest headed south.

"We might be able to help them with the wounded, Gunner. We know some pretty good doctoring Mother taught us."

Avery knew he'd run out of daylight soon. He tried to shake these events out of his mind and the anger from his heart; his head throbbed with conflicting emotion. Saddened by the dead and injured soldiers, he raged against those who were entertained by the soldiers' miseries. He breathed deeply as his father had taught him and folded his hands together in prayer. Feeling calmer and more relaxed, he whistled to his dog, and they moved on.

Gunner jogged down the hill; Avery kept up, and they headed east to the turnpike. Once he got past the hill, he was aware of noise and movement and realized he was moving parallel with one of the armies from the skirmish in the glen. *Which one?* he wondered. They straggled out of the woods in front of him, heading for the turnpike.

Avery fell back and waited. Soon they were in front of him, behind him, and all around him. The smell of powder reached Gunner's nose, and the gun dog was on alert. The caisson creaked and groaned, and the ground trembled under them; moans and groans echoed from the ambulance wagons. Riders came out of the woods and joined the rear.

It all seemed terribly disorganized to Avery. There was no marching to the cadence of a drum and fife, only a haphazard shuffling of worn boots and tired legs. There were no smart uniforms. The soldiers wore an assortment of uniforms, mostly torn and ragged. There were no battalion flags flying proudly in the breeze, only a flag of the Union of States painted on the side of one of the wagons. The officers on horseback were wearing dirty, dusty, Union blue.

"Well, Gunner, it looks like we just joined the Union Army. What do you say about that?" Gunner cocked his head, picked his feet up smartly, and pranced into the middle of the disheveled men.

When the order was given to *Halt!*, it was nearly dark. Amidst moans and groans, the men broke their ranks and collapsed on the ground. One of the officers on a large gray mule rode among them, speaking in a loud voice. Avery estimated there were only a few hundred men he was addressing. *Not much of an army*, he thought.

The officer sat tall in his saddle. "I appreciate your bravery, soldiers, and though it was a small battle, it was important for the Union. I'm proud of all of you. Make camp and man your stations." They groaned, but they obeyed.

Avery and Gunner watched with interest from a distance. It reminded Avery of a honey bee colony with every worker knowing just what to do. No other orders were given, but A-tents were popping up in orderly lines. Men built cooking fires, aligned the wagons, and tethered the horses in the woods. They felled trees to feed the fires, tended the wounded in the hospital tent, and served supper. It all seemed so well rehearsed. Avery and Gunner were fascinated.

Avery expected that the exhausted soldiers would go to their tents immediately. But following the quiet supper of Burnside stew and corn dodgers, the soldiers seemed to get their second wind. Avery heard the musical notes of a harmonica, and someone began to sing along. A soldier plunked a mouth harp; a tin whistle and hand claps joined him. Men made up rhymes about the Confederacy, and everyone laughed. They played games of Bird Cage and Chuck-a-Luck by the firelight. Some played checkers, using checkerboards drawn on the muslin side of their rainproof ponchos. Avery set up his tarpaulin shelter at the edge of the woods and spread his rubber sheet on the ground. He and Gunner crawled inside, shared some hardtack, and unnoticed by the soldiers, fell asleep listening to their music.

CHAPTER NINE
UNION BLUE

Avery was up at dawn when he heard the cook's tent coming alive. He slipped off into the woods to take care of his private business and returned eating a handful of blackberries. He and Gunner approached the kitchen wagon.

"Good morning," he said in his extra friendly and polite voice.

"Who're you?" asked the gruff soldier cook. "I ain't seen you here before."

"I'm Avery Junior Bennett, sir. I can help you with the cooking, if you'd like some help. All I'm asking in return is the use of your fire to cook me and my dog some breakfast."

"Wait just a minute here. Who'd you say you were? You stay right here. Sentry!" Immediately a soldier was in front of Avery with his gun pointed directly at him.

"Major General Keese," the soldier yelled out over his shoulder. "Someone get the general. We got us a spy." Five more soldiers came on the run in various stages of dress, some wearing only their underdrawers, all carrying their guns now pointed at Avery.

"What's going on here?" It was the tall officer Avery had seen last evening on the mule.

"A spy, sir. Came creeping in here right past the sentries. Says he can help cook if I let him use the fire. Likely story. He ain't one of us, that's for sure." The cook spat on the ground.

The tall officer faced Avery, and said, "Well, what do you say for yourself?"

But Avery was more interested in the guns pointing at him.

"Are you planning to shoot me?" he asked the first man simply. "Because if you aren't, you need to point your gun to the ground. You shouldn't aim your gun unless you plan to use it. That's the first rule of responsible gun ownership; my father told me that."

Avery stood tall and confident. He was already as tall as some of the shorter men. The man's face reddened as the rest broke into laughter at his expense. The red-faced cook's mouth took on a hard line. The cook took a step toward Avery.

"Let it go, Richardson. At ease, all of you," commanded the officer.

"Anything goes missing out of my stores, we'll know who to blame, and then we'll see about pointing this gun," spat Richardson, the cook. "I'll be making my own rules about that."

"Enough, Richardson. Who are you, boy, and what do you want? State your business."

I'm Avery Junior Bennett, sir, and I'm from Kanawha Valley. This is my dog, Gunner. We're on an errand to find my uncle, Fredric Lennemann, who went to the war. He's needed at home, and I came to fetch him. Well, if I can find him, that is. That's all I'm about, sir. If anyone here knows about him, I'd be obliged if they'd tell me. I've got my own rations, and I'd just like to camp and eat. I mean to be no bother."

General Keese looked around at the befuddled men and laughed aloud.

"Yes, I can see you men have yourselves a spy indeed. You're well spoken, Avery Junior Bennett, and you're welcome at our camp. No one will bother you. Come to the fire and have some hot coffee. Richardson?"

Avery was handed a steaming mug and said, "Thank you," politely to the grizzled cook.

"Thank you," mimicked the cook in a sarcastic, squeaky little voice.

"Tell me about yourself, Mr. Bennett, and the Kanawha Valley."

"There's not much to me, sir, and you can call me Avery. I'm fourteen years old, and I had schooling by my mother, Sarah Littlefield Bennett, who is very educated. And I'm a good shot at squirrels, rabbits, and birds. Kanawha is a nice valley, and all the folks there are peaceable. I'm just looking for Fredric Lennemann, who is somewhere in the army."

"I understand Kanawha is seceding from Virginia to become the State of Kanawha, favorable to the Union of States," offered the general.

"Really? My father was called to a meeting in Wheeling to talk about it all, but I didn't know what they figured out to do. The State of Kanawha?"

"I read in a paper that the more popular choice of name is West Virginia, Kanawha being the choice of some of the local folks."

"Well, I'm glad you told me that, I sure didn't know about that. I learned all the states in the United States and their capital cities and how to spell them all and how to find them on the map. Guess I'll know this one the best. But it looks like a lot might be changing; I might need to learn it all over again," Avery said thoughtfully.

After supper that evening, the general came back and sat by Avery and Gunner.

"Tell me about your family, Avery." The general seemed eager for conversation, and even though Avery was tired, he obliged. He sipped his coffee and listened to the camp quieting down. While he talked about his family, he was aware of snoring all around him. The officer continued to question him with interest.

"Dr. Clayton Littlefield of Boston, you say? He was your grandfather? I knew him; I'm from Boston. He was a great man, Dr. Littlefield. He was the best doctor Boston ever had."

Avery was astonished at this news. "You knew my grandfather? Really? And did you know my mother? She's Sarah Phoebe Littlefield Bennett."

"Indeed I did," smiled the soldier. "Indeed I did, and her sister, the lovely Miss Caroline Littlefield."

"Aunt Caroline? You knew Aunt Caroline in Boston? It's Aunt Caroline's husband that I'm on errand to find. Sir, you didn't give me your name. I'll remember you to Aunt Caroline and my mother when I get back home."

"I apologize for my field manners, Avery. Seems I've been out of polite company for too long. My name is Geoffrey Keese. Major General Geoffrey Keese, Army of the Potomac, U.S. Army." They shook hands and called it a day.

In his tarpaulin tent, lying on his rubber sheet, feet sticking out one end and head looking at the stars out the other, Avery thought about home. Gunner stretched out next to him under the cover of the tarpaulin. Avery stroked the hound dog's head. He wondered if his mother and father would be happy with how well he and Gunner had fared so far. He thought he'd used good manners and good judgment. His temper had been tested but kept under control. He decided they'd approve of how well they were getting along. He fell asleep saying his prayers. He dreamed about Aunt Caroline, his mother, Boston (the city he'd never seen), the grandfather he didn't know, and a red-haired girl he'd spoken to once.

In the morning Richardson approached Avery and thrust a large gunny sack into his surprised arms.

"General Keese says you was to git two weeks rations for you and the mutt. Man's crazy. You take this, and you git on yer way."

Avery had no idea why Richardson hated him so much. "Wonder what we did to him, Gunner? Father read to us not to repay evil with evil or snap back at those who are unkind. I guess I should pray for Richardson today. Maybe God can lighten his burden of hate."

He packed his gear, shook hands with General Keese, thanked him, and whistled for Gunner. From the darkness of the woods, he heard a horse whinny. It was an anxious whinny, repeated over and over getting more persistent, followed by the stamping of hooves. Other horses began to react, and the whinny-ing became a chorus. Gunner had reacted to the first whinny and was already racing into the woods, bellowing.

"Hey! Get that dog out of there!" yelled the soldiers, bolt-ing after Gunner.

"It's okay," yelled Avery. "He's good with horses; he'll be okay. Don't worry." Avery was running pell-mell through the thicket to catch up with Gunner, who obviously was on a mission of his own, bellowing his hound-dog best.

"Fool dog's probably stampeding them. I knew those two was trouble," spat out Richardson, but he didn't move to go after them. The quartermaster, who'd been doling out the oat rations, dropped his work and ran to settle the horses.

Deep in the dense woods, the horses were tethered to the pine trees. The snickering, stamping horse, practically yodeling with her head bobbing up and down, was tethered in the center of the treed corral. She rubbed her neck against Gunner, who licked her muzzle while his tail waved wildly.

"Get the dog away," commanded the quartermaster. But in a moment the men saw what was happening with the horse quietly coddling the dog; they were so astonished they said nothing more and stared.

It was Avery who shouted loud and clear, "Fan!" He ran stumbling to the horse, and threw his arms around her neck.

"Get away from that horse," yelled the quartermaster. "You fool kid, you'll get yourself killed!" But Avery didn't hear any of them. The dog, the horse, and the boy were locked in a single happy embrace. Avery felt tears rising in his eyes. He stepped back and began to check each of the horse's hooves. He had no idea what he was checking for, but he was certain that his father would've done this, and it was something to do; the tears were awkward. He didn't want the soldiers to think he was a crybaby.

"What are you doing? Leave that horse alone!" He heard the soldiers yelling at him, but all he said was, "Oh, Fan, I never thought I'd see you again, girl." Gunner, with his happy tail wav-ing, licked the horse's lips. Fan snorted joyfully.

"What's going on here, Bennett?" It was General Keese.

Thank goodness, thought Avery. The general appeared with a small bunch of soldiers who were in various stages of dressing, shaving, and eating.

"This is my horse, sir. This is my horse, Fan." Avery felt his throat constricting, and his eyes glistened with tears. "She heard me whistle for Gunner, and she let Gunner know where she was. Gunner could find Fan in an entire herd of horses. See? They sleep in the same stall." He pointed to the nuzzling animals, Gunner still licking the muzzle of the contented horse, whose head bobbed up and down caressing the hound's shoulder.

The officer could see that Avery was telling the truth; animals don't lie. "Soldier, how did this horse come to be here?" he asked the quartermaster.

"Don't know, Sir. I imagine it was sequestered with the rest."

"She was *borrowed* off our farm by marauders along with a lot of other stock and food. The soldiers said *borrowed*. My father says it's not our place to judge, but I think it was more like stolen." Avery felt his temper surging just thinking about that day.

"You listen here, boy. I told you to git." It was Richardson coming into the wooded clearing, shaking his fist at him.

"Bennett, was your family given a sequestration receipt from the army for all the sequestered goods?"

"No, sir."

"My apologies to your family. Quartermaster, prepare this horse for travel. Two weeks rations in the panniers. Put a McClellan saddle on her. Consider it a gift, Avery, from the United States government to thank you for the loan of your fine horse. I want an A-tent and a bed roll on that saddle."

The men stood gaping; they wanted to argue.

"*NOW*, soldiers," he ordered. When the soldiers were gone, Avery moved back to his horse and his dog, hugging and caressing them both.

"How did you come by this fine horse, Bennett?" the general asked nicely as he stroked the horse's neck.

"I helped my father bring her into this life. Her mama had considerable trouble foaling, and we all stayed with her all night. My mother tried every kind of medicine, but the mare died anyway. Fan was born with this little white medallion on her forehead that looks like tatted lace. See this?" He lifted her thick forelock, and the officer nodded.

"I said she looked fancy, and that's what I called her, Fancy. I nursed her, walked her, and cared for her, and I even slept with her in the barn so she wouldn't miss her mama so much. She thrived, and my father said she was mine. Gunner has shared the stall with her since he was just a pup."

"She's a good horse. You're fine at animal husbandry, Avery Junior Bennett, and I bet your father is mighty proud to be your father."

"Thank you, sir. I hope so, sir."

He hoped he wasn't being prideful, but it felt awfully good to hear the kind words from the general. He was missing his father's reassurances.

"Let's get some boots on your feet, Mr. Bennett." He smiled at the toes of the boy's worn stockings sticking out through his open-toed boots.

The pair of boots that Avery was given were funny looking, and he wasn't quite sure how to go about wearing them. One of the soldiers saw his puzzlement.

"They're called crooked shoes. Both feet are just alike. When one wears out, you can filch another from a dead soldier, who won't need it, and not worry about which shoe it is. Pretty handy, don't you say?"

Avery pulled them on and was surprised to see that they did, indeed, work as a fine set. He couldn't imagine replacing one with a shoe from a dead soldier. But he reasoned, it probably wasn't like stealing, more like not wasting since the soldier wouldn't have further need of them. By midday everything was readied, and Avery, Gunner, and Fan headed off to the turnpike once again.

"Sure feels good to not be walking, Fan," he said to his horse. "Thanks again, Gunner."

CHAPTER TEN

TRAPPED

They traveled until late afternoon, and when they came upon a forested glen along a stream, Avery decided to set up their camp early. It looked like a reasonable place to find game and fish. There was a blanket of soft moss, level ground, shade from the heat, and cover for safety; this would be perfect.

He went through his regular routine of setting up camp, which by now was so mechanical that he didn't give it much thought; he just did it. But today he would try out a new idea that one of the blacksmithing soldiers had showed him. Avery liked new ideas and was always keen to try out any new invention.

Using one of the food tins and a horseshoe nail to puncture it full of holes, he'd placed some hot glowing coals in the tin to be kept alive to light his next fire. He hoped it would work as well as the soldiers' fire keepers worked. The coal seemed to be dead out, but as he blew lightly the way they showed him, the coal began to glow; he used it to light his next fire.

"Well," he said to Gunner, "today it was me, rather than you, who learned a new trick. This is a pretty good invention, this fire keeper. Maybe someday we'll invent something to help people." Gunner went on with his own important business of sniffing trees and grasses.

It was while they were supping on fried cornmeal and dandelion greens that Avery thought he heard something, kind of a wailing sound. Gunner stood up, his ears on alert. Quietly Avery stood and reached for his musket. He leaned his back against the tree and waited. He heard the wail again. In the woods it's hard to tell exactly where a sound is coming from, so he watched Gunner orient, knowing that the dog had his own compass. He wasn't looking to the trees; it wasn't an owl. Gunner began to pace his eager hound-dog prance, staring into the pine stand. *Perhaps a mountain lion*, Avery thought; *it could be the mournful wail of a panther.* He considered his twitching dog and hoped not.

"Sh," Avery ordered Gunner and Fan. "Sh." Again they heard the long moan.

"Gunner, easy; find it." Gunner knew the command. Nose to the ground, he went to work. Periodically he sniffed the air. He stopped and listened, then nose back to the ground. He was on the track; Avery could tell by his ears and tail. He followed quietly about ten feet behind the dog. If he needed to get a shot off, he'd need to have an angle of safety for his dog. Fan stamped impatiently wanting to be included. It was darker in the woods than Avery had anticipated. Air scenting, Gunner moved confidently and quickly. Avery knew they were close because of the excitement he could read in his hound. The occasional moan grew louder. Gunner suddenly shot forward with a bellow and ran the last few yards. Dodging trees and trying to keep up, Avery held his musket safely and ready. Having reached his quarry, Gunner was circling and braying, his tail stiff behind him, keeping his prey under guard until Avery was near and could take over. A loud moan wafted to Avery's ears, and Gunner was hard at work, excited and pleased with himself.

"Good boy, Gunner. Thank you," He studied the ground next to his feet trying to figure out what he was looking at. Whatever it was, it wasn't trying to get away.

"Gunner, off." Gunner came to his side, tail wagging, and sat.

The ragged and nearly unconscious soldier was lying in an unnatural and contorted position. Avery studied him from his head to his shoulders and arms. All his limbs were accounted for, and there was no fresh blood. Avery's eyes adjusted to the darkness, and they followed down his body to his legs, to his— and then he saw it.

"Oh, no! Oh, no, Gunner, we have to help him." Avery inhaled. "Oh, God, you must help me to help this man. Tell me what to do." The man's ankle was locked in the jaws of a very cruel trap. It was a sort that Avery's father wouldn't allow on his property. "Cruel and Inhumane" was the name of this trap, according to his father. He'd taught Avery how to release the trap in the event he ever came upon one. But he cautioned him that if he found an animal locked in one of these, he'd have to put the animal out of its misery before he could release the trap. So cruel was this trap, the animal would die with much pain and suffering if he were released. Better that he be relieved of suffering immediately, his father had cautioned. Avery hoped he'd never see one of these traps again. But here it was, and the pain and suffering were already evident.

He rolled the man onto his back so that the trapped leg was straightened out, and he could see the damage. He tried to spring the trap, but the locking screw and spring were rusty and wouldn't budge. The dried blood made it difficult to see the screw, and he was glad the soldier was mostly unconscious.

"Gunner, I have to get some things, boy. Stay." Avery ran back through the woods, following the smell of his wood fire. He grabbed his knapsack, his Bowie knife, tarpaulin, canteen, and lantern and ran back toward the dark woods. He heard a flutter in the trees and looked up to see three buzzards spreading their wings, preparing to move in on their prey.

"Gunner!" he called, when he realized he wasn't sure of the way. He heard the dog racing across the forest floor, and in seconds Gunner was leading him back to the trapped soldier. Gunner leaped, snarling, dispersing the buzzards as they tried to land on the unconscious soldier.

Avery lit the lantern and set it next to the trap. Taking his Bowie knife out of the sheath, he worked the screw, which held the spring that held the cruel iron teeth deep into the man's mangled ankle. When the screw suddenly released, the spring uncoiled, and the jaws of the trap sprang open, tearing the flesh around the wounds and restarting the bleeding that had clotted and dried. The man moaned again but didn't move. Avery lifted the leg carefully and slid the circular jaws off the leg. He wanted to give it a hateful toss, but it was so heavy that he could hardly lift it at all.

"Who would use such a terrible trap for anything?" he almost shouted, as he dragged the heavy iron trap.

Avery washed the wound and bound it to stop the bleeding. He rolled the man onto his tarpaulin, and dragged him through the woods. He was glad the man wasn't fully conscious, as this would've been an added misery for him. Next to the firelight, Avery washed the wounds more thoroughly and packed them with his mother's poultice for drawing out infection. He covered the man and tried to get him to take some water; he checked on him throughout the night. He washed the wounds and repacked them with fresh poultices every few hours. He was certain the ankle bone was broken.

In the morning the soldier was hot with fever. All day long, Avery tended to him, using everything he could think of in his mother's tin of medicines. *What if I forget and use the wrong one? What if I make the man sicker? What if he dies?* Avery prayed throughout the day and continued to tend the fevered patient and his wound, packing it, cleaning it, and drawing out infection.

In two days the fever was gone, and the man was drinking broth. His wound looked clean. Avery kept a poultice packed in it with the leg elevated. He kept it clean and changed the bandages frequently. On the fifth day he felt the man was strong enough to travel. Avery made a litter out of tree limbs and his tarpaulin. The man was able to help get himself onto the litter. Using her reins, he attached the frame to Fan, and she walked beside Avery and Gunner. Avery figured that General Keese's company was still a day or two behind him, so off they went back to the encampment.

"What in thunder is that?" the sentries said, when they saw the strange entourage.

"Halt! Who goes there?" called out the first posted sentry.

"*What* goes there?" wondered the second sentry.

"It's me. Avery Junior Bennett."

"State your business."

"I need to see Major General Keese right away."

"Stay right there."

The second sentry said, "It's that meddlesome kid again with the dog. Who knows what kind of mischief he wants now. Keese gave him some of our rations, like we have some to spare." The soldier spat on the ground in annoyance.

"General's busy. Can't see nobody."

"He'll see me. Just tell him, please."

"Just tell him, please," they mimicked sarcastically in little baby voices. "Just tell him please, please, and pretty please," they mocked.

"Get lost kid!"

Avery told Gunner to stay with Fan, and he quietly flanked the campground.

When he was close enough to the headquarter tent, he yelled, "General Keese! General Keese! It's me, Avery, and I need to see you!" The startled encampment ran to their positions.

"Show yourself!" called out the aide-de-camp. "Hands up and walk slowly."

Avery put his hands on his head and walked into the encampment.

"How did you get past the sentinels?" the aide asked him, when he saw who it was.

"Quietly, sir," smiled Avery.

"Wait here." The aide came back promptly with General Keese.

"Avery Junior Bennett! What brings you back to our camp?"

Avery blurted out his story. "He's real sick, and I've been doctoring him about five days and nights, and he needs your doctor; he's a soldier, sir."

"Davis, Pristus, James, get a detail together and follow Bennett."

"Thank you, sir, I'm grateful."

The man was put into the hospital tent, and when everyone

had gone about his business, the camp surgeon and the general joined Avery and Gunner at the camp supper. The physician told the general what a fine job Avery had done.

"Most men caught in that trap would have their leg gone to gangrene or died fighting it," he said. "This man will recover, thanks to Avery." The physician wondered how Avery knew about poultices and how to cleanse the wound. He was amazed to learn that he was fourteen years old; he was impressed with Avery's skill and knowledge.

"Ever think about being a doctor, lad?"

"Yes, sir. I've given it some thought and prayer."

"He's a remarkable lad," the doctor said.

"Yes," agreed the general, "remarkable."

The next morning, Avery, Gunner, and Fan left the encampment for the second time and headed for the turnpike.

"Let's go find Uncle Fredric, Gunner. And maybe we can help some other soldiers along the way."

Morning after morning, Avery broke camp and walked the turnpike with Fan and Gunner. They paused in the forests to rest, eat, and forage; they rested along the river to drink, wash, and fish, and then slept under the stars in their army-issue A-tent. The weather had been favorable for travel since the long month of summer rain. The days were growing shorter, the nights longer and chillier. The leaves were starting to change color, and they fluttered crisply to the forest floor like tired butterflies. Gentle breezes blew them across the turnpike, Gunner chasing them merrily zigzagging down the pike.

Passing through valley after valley, holler after holler, Avery saw the signs everywhere of a country at war. He saw farms where hay wasn't mowed, cornfields broken and burned, and tasseled ears not harvested. He put some of these ears of corn from abandoned farms into his panniers. Not stealing, he told himself, just not wasting—like the crooked shoes. He saw family laundry hanging on clotheslines at neglected farm houses. Skirts and children's clothing blew in the autumn breezes, but no britches or men's shirts hung on the clotheslines.

He picked berries and mushrooms, sucked on honey-suckle, and cracked hickory nuts. He gathered feverfew, mustard, and other medicinal plants to dry and store for future use.

They passed columns of soldiers moving down the turn-pike, but the countryside was otherwise ghostly quiet. How much longer, he wondered, until he found Uncle Fredric and he could go back home? In the distance he heard mortar and cannon; there was a lot of smoke on the horizon. *More injured and dead soldiers,* he thought. Avery and Gunner walked on.

CHAPTER ELEVEN

BRILLIANT INVENTIONS

After several uneventful days, he began to see more traffic on the turnpike and guessed that he might be coming upon a city or a depot. Pausing for food and water, he stretched out in the grass and looked up into the bright blue sky of autumn. He bolted upright.

"What is that?" he blurted aloud. He cupped his eyes against the azure sky. There above him was a huge, shining ball that appeared to be flying and hovering like a bird. Avery had never seen or heard of such a thing. Gunner sat beside him and stared, while Fan munched contentedly on the roadside grasses. They watched in amazement for a while until it seemed to be falling down from the sky. Avery's curiosity had reached its limit.

"Come on." He took off running with Gunner beside him and confused Fan trotting along on the end of her rein.

A crowd of people was gathering at the roadside with soldiers, horses, tents, and wagons. Avery couldn't imagine what this was all about. There in the clearing, the huge ball was coming down. As he watched the women and children, town people, and farmers, he realized that he could mingle in this crowd without notice. He watched in amazement as the huge ball hit the ground.

Everyone applauded when two soldiers and a nicely dressed gentleman exited from the large wicker basket that was attached to the ball. Avery rubbed his eyes; maybe he was dreaming. Two other soldiers got into the basket with some equipment and writing papers. The ball gave out a loud roar, bobbed around, and lifted off the ground. The crowd applauded.

"Ever seen anything like this before?" The nicely dressed man was standing next to Avery and speaking to him.

"Oh, no, sir, I never did," Avery answered him with a voice filled with awe and amazement, his eyes on the ball. Gunner stared, ears back.

"It's a hydrogen-gas balloon, boy. Brilliant, isn't it?"

"Yes, sir, it is. What is it? I mean, what's it for? What are they doing? How does it work?"

"It belongs to Thaddeus Lowe. He has a special company of balloons that are part of the Union army. A balloon corps, of all things; brilliant, I tell you, just brilliant. This one is called *The Intrepid*. They go up there and spy on the enemy. Heh, heh, just brilliant, yes, siree. They check the weather from up there too. Right now they're looking for a company of Confederates somewhere in those hills over there. They'll make some maps of the area and pinpoint the camp. And that's not all. They can send telegraphs from up there to direct artillery fire. Brilliant, I tell you, brilliant! The kind of intelligence that'll win this war."

Avery watched the hot-air balloon for the rest of the day. By the time most of the people left and the afternoon cooled down, he realized he'd lost an entire travel day without making any inquiries about Uncle Fredric.

"Tomorrow, Gunner and Fan, we have to march double time." He watched the men deflate the balloon and roll it up. The basket, the balloon, and all the tethers were packed into the specially made wagon, and they pulled away down the road. Avery pitched his tent. He and Gunner ate cold food without benefit of a fire while Fan grazed.

"That was a pretty amazing invention, huh, Gunner? Wouldn't a ride in that be something? I must tell everyone about it when I write a letter home." Avery fell asleep trying to imagine what the world would look like from the airborne balloon, looking down at the tops of the trees.

True to his word, the next morning they were up early

and covered several miles, stopping only for food and water. By sundown they reached the outpost of a large Union encampment. Avery presented himself and said he carried a message to their ranking officer from Major General Keese.

The sentry called from his post, "Official Army Courier, let him pass."

Well, I didn't know I was an official army courier; that sounds kind of important. When he had left the general's camp, he carried a letter in an envelope with the general's seal on it. The general had told him to present it at any camp and say it was from him, and he'd be well received.

The ranking officer made Avery welcome for supper and told the horse guard to feed and quarter Fan. Avery pitched his official army A-tent. In the morning the officer told Avery they'd be moving out within twenty-four hours for Alexandria. If he'd like to travel with them, he'd be welcome. Gunner had already met most of the soldiers.

"Alexandria? Do you think it will be a good place to find my uncle?"

"Good a place as any. They'll be a lot of soldiers to ask."

Avery considered it and decided it would be good to have some company for a change. He learned to play cards and dice games of chance; he laughed at their jokes and shared some of his father's riddles. He learned to sing some songs and recite poems. He made himself useful by helping some of the soldiers with bandages, wound care, headaches, toothaches, bee stings, and rashes. Word traveled quickly through the camp that if you had a health problem or an injury, young Bennett was the *doctor* to see. The company enjoyed Gunner's tricks and laughed at the story of how they used his trick to run off the marauders. Avery thought Gunner looked like he was putting on some weight.

Once in a while, Avery regretted his decision to travel with the slow-moving company. He knew he could make better time if he were alone. But every day was an opportunity to inquire about Fredric Lennemann.

"Moving an army is as slow as a turtle," he complained

impatiently. "They're carrying everything with them." They often stopped to wait for the heavy, slow artillery wagons to catch up. But the officers told him that the farther east they traveled, the more dangerous the journey would become; the likelihood of meeting rebel resistance increased by the mile. He talked to many men in the company and inquired if anyone had heard of Fredric Lennemann. No one had.

"You sure he's not in the Confederate Army?" someone teased him. Avery was taken aback. Was he sure? Well, the truth be told, he really didn't know; he just assumed he would find him with the Union somewhere in Virginia. But he was learning that Virginia was a big place. He was sure he would find him some-time, somewhere.

One afternoon, as they were setting up their camp for the night, a strange-looking square, black, enclosed wagon approached them. Soldiers drifted out to the sentries' posts to have a look. Avery had never seen such a peculiar looking wagon, and everyone else seemed very interested too. One of the sentries approached the wagon and discussed something with the driver before looking over his shoulder at Avery.

"Fetch the captain," the sentry said.

"Sure!" Avery went off on a run, pleased to be asked to do something useful.

Captain Greene, Avery, and Gunner accompanied the wagon into the camp, followed by the curious soldiers. Avery walked around the wagon and tried to peek around the black cur-tains. The side of the wagon had fancy lettering on it in gold and red and said *Mathew Brady Company, New York, Photographer.*

The soldiers milled about the campfire; some put on their uniforms and spiffed up a bit.

"Hello there, my young fellow," said a nicely dressed man with a top hat. "Who are you, may I ask?"

"I'm Avery Junior Bennett. I'm an official army courier."

"Well, then, Mr. Bennett, official army courier, we'd best make your official likeness here for posterity. Now, let's see, hmm. How about right over here? Stand right here. Put one foot on this stump and stand tall. Look over this way. Here, put this hand here, just like this." He laid one of Avery's hands across his chest.

Avery felt pretty silly standing there posed like a stuffed turkey.

"What do you think, Gunner? Do I look as silly as I feel?"

"Okay now, chest out, stand tall, and put your eyes on this, over here." The photographer disappeared under a black cloth. Gunner came to Avery's side and sat posing.

"Where'd that dog come from?" the man sputtered as he emerged from under his cover.

"It's my dog, sir."

"Well, move him!" barked the busy man, disappearing under the hood to peer through the camera.

"He'd like to be in your picture too," said Avery.

"I think you should include him," smiled the captain. "Avery wouldn't look much like himself without Gunner at his side. He's more recognizable with his dog."

"Oh well, have it your way then." He lined them up, checked the shadows, and after considerable formalities, he squeezed the bulb.

"Sir?" asked Avery, "Could you make a likeness of my horse? My father and mother would like to see that I have her."

"Unusual," grumbled the photographer. "Unusual lad, but I try to be accommodating to my customers." So after going through more photographer rituals, Avery Junior Bennett, Gunner, and Fancy all had their images recorded for posterity.

The photographer hung around camp for a couple of days, traveling with them by day and camping by night, coming and going out of his mysterious black wagon, lining up the soldiers, positioning hats and props, and being, as he liked to say, accommodating.

By suppertime of the third day, he was inviting soldiers to his wagon and handing out little pictures called ambrotypes, "for all posterity," he said over and over. Most of them sat on a display so the soldiers could find their own.

Avery gazed in amazement at his image. He recognized

smiling Gunner and Fan of course, but he was surprised by his own image. Except for an occasional glimpse of his face reflected in a river or stream, Avery had been quite unaware of his own appearance. He studied the little ambrotype realizing this was how others saw him. He was startled to see that he looked quite a bit like both his father and his brother. The photographer opened his palm and stood waiting for payment. Avery didn't notice him, as he continued to stare at the little images. The photographer scratched his head and waited impatiently to be paid. The captain stepped up behind the photographer and put two Union chits in his hand and sent him on his way to the next soldier. Avery didn't take his eyes off the images.

Later that evening, Captain Greene explained to Avery how he could post the ambrotypes to his family back in Kanawha for no cost.

"Soldiers use a two-letter code instead of a postage stamp. You may have that code, since you're an official army courier." He winked at Avery and handed him a little note pad, a pen, and ink. Avery wrote his first letter home.

Somewhere on the Turnpike

Late in the Summer

Dear Mother and Father, Aunt Caroline, and Clayton, if he has come home yet,

This is a picture of me with Gunner and Fan. Gunner found Fan with soldiers, and we got her back. She has a new McClellan saddle. The picture was taken by Mr. O'Sullivan, who works for Mathew Brady's Photography Company. He is a famous photographer who has many photographers working for him. They visit soldier encampments and battlefields.

Will the family think I look like Father?

I hope all of you are well. Gunner and I are doing very well, I think.

Mother will like to hear that.

I have seen the whole world, just about. I've seen soldiers flying in a gas balloon over the hillsides, eaten strange army foods, and learned some new riddles, games, and songs. I can almost recite the entire poem of "All Quiet on the Potomac Tonight" by Ethel Lynn Beers. Have you heard that before? The soldiers like it.

I met a friend, Major General Geoffrey Keese, who is from Boston and is a long ago friend of Aunt Caroline and knows you, Mother. He sends his regards to all of you. He is very nice and has been a help to me.

I have helped in the camps to care for the sick and wounded, and when we get to Alexandria, Captain Greene says I can get a real job at one of the many army hospitals. General Keese says I have a calling

like grandfather to be a healer. Maybe that is so.
When I get to the hospitals, there will be many
soldiers whom I can ask about Uncle Fredric. Don't
worry, Aunt Caroline, I promise I will find him. I
look forward to bringing us all home before the end of
this year.

The captain says the war is a long ways till over
yet, but things are quiet here as we move on towards
Alexandria. I'll write you a letter again when I get
there.

Our regards to all of you,

Avery Junior Bennett, Gunner, and Fan

Avery read his letter and checked for any misspelled words. His mother would find them if he didn't. He signed his name with his best penmanship to please his father.

The letter and the ambrotypes went into a little brown parcel; and with the special two-letter code, it was on its way traveling free by U.S. Post all the way back to the Kanawha Valley, from which he'd departed; it seemed so long ago.

CHAPTER TWELVE

DESTINATIONS

The march to Alexandria was mostly uneventful and slow. Occasional skirmishes with a few maverick rebels broke the monotony but never amounted to much. They marched; they sang; they ate; they camped. Two more companies, including Major General Keese's regiment, had joined the camp. Avery thought they were beginning to look like a real army. He was happy to see his friend General Keese again.

One night they camped along the edge of a marsh. Except for the aggravation of mosquitoes, Avery enjoyed the sights and the sounds of the marsh. Gunner was thoroughly enjoying the change of scenery, and his senses were keen. Avery was amused, watching Gunner on his adventures, tracking prey known only to the dog and reading the history of their trails. As dawn broke the next morning, Avery was awakened by the familiar sound of honking geese. He bolted out of his bedroll; and with Gunner leading the way, he grabbed his musket and beat a trek into the marsh.

He marveled, as he always did, at the beautiful formation of the geese. He and Gunner waited patiently for the watery approach and landing of the geese. Honking with glee, the first goose dropped from the sky and skidded across the glassy marsh pond, followed by the next and the next. Gracefully the formation slid, as if on ice, across the still pond. He watched in appreciation of the graceful and beautiful geese before him.

"Steady, Gunner," he whispered. "Steady, Avery," he

reminded himself. The relaxed, unhurried flock glided past the hunter, honking and socializing. Avery steadied himself against one of the few stumps in the marsh. He stayed low in the tall marsh grasses. He took careful aim, making a slight adjustment, knowing his gun.

"Steady, Gunner." The geese were beautiful; he hated what he was about to do. The musket exploded into the quiet morning, and the sound echoed across the marsh.

"Go, Gunner!"

All the geese lifted off, honking in confusion—all but one. Gunner was on the way. He hurled himself into the water, swimming effortlessly toward the lone goose that was tilting and bobbing in the water. He dragged the huge goose through the water to the shore, where Avery helped him pull it out onto solid ground.

"Good boy, Gunner. Thanks, boy." Avery said a thankful prayer, as his father always did, *for the bounty in our life*. He patted his dog, picked the goose up by its legs, and tossed it over his shoulder. He was surprised at how heavy it was. He carried his musket in the other hand as he and Gunner walked back to camp, which was now bustling and reacting to the sound of musket fire. Sentries were in position. Everyone relaxed when they saw that Avery, his dog, and musket had been hunting. Avery carried the heavy goose to the mess tent, where he knew the cooks would be in their morning grump, especially Richardson. He walked up to the cook and squared himself toe to toe.

"I have something for you," he said to Richardson. He swung the goose around and pushed it into the surprised man's arms. The astonished cook was ready to spew oaths until he realized what he was holding. His jaw dropped, his eyes nearly popped out of his head, and slowly but surely a huge grin split his mellowing face from ear to ear.

"Gunner gets the neck and the giblets," Avery said with authority. Feeling satisfied, he left the mess tent. He hoped the cook would feel more favorably disposed toward him and Gunner after the next fine meal. He went back to his tent and washed up for the day. In a short while, he spotted Gunner lying in the grass under the trees. The dog gnawed happily on the neck and feasted on the giblets.

"You're welcome, Gunner."

At camp that evening, while they enjoyed their hearty meal of fresh meat, the general gave them the welcome news that tomorrow they would be in Alexandria. The news was greeted with cheers.

Alexandria lay before them. Avery's heart beat an extra hard thump when he saw the city. Until now it had only been the name of a faraway place, a dot on his map, the name of their destination. Virginia was a big state, bigger than he'd ever imagined. But now he could see church steeples and smoking chimneys. Alexandria, Virginia, was a real place.

The soldiers marched along the edge of the town, trying to look like a professional army, rather than a tired and dirty ragtag collection of hurting, homesick men. The men were in battle-ready formation, and they were impressive by their numbers. Some people along the way clapped, and children ran joyfully alongside them. Avery wondered if they were really glad to see them or if they were just clamoring to see a battle. *Maybe they'll have a picnic*, he thought bitterly. His mouth tasted sour at that remembrance.

As they moved through the streets, Avery could see that Alexandria was an old city with fine houses, shops, and churches. He saw that many of the large homes, warehouses, and churches were being used by the Union Army units for headquarters, army offices, barracks, and hospitals.

He walked, leading Fan, and enjoyed taking in the sights at his leisure. Gunner sniffed the surroundings excitedly. One of the soldiers walking near Avery commented that many Alexandrians had abandoned these houses last spring when the Union Army came to occupy the city. Those leaning to the Confederacy followed Confederate soldiers out of town. Those who stayed swore oaths of allegiance to the Union.

"Did you know that George Washington was born here? He helped lay out the streets. It's pretty historical around here.

Ever been here before?"

"No." Avery gazed all around. There was no singing, no gaming going on here; they were all soldiering. It was their duty to protect the nearby capital from enemy advances. The encampment of the Confederacy was only one hundred miles away in Richmond. The next morning at the earliest light, General Keese awakened Avery and told him to pack his gear.

Avery did as he was told without questioning. He gulped a mug of coffee and mounted up. Fan was already fed and saddled with her new saddle. A party of four soldiers appeared from the mist and closed rank. The six of them headed north away from the camp. They walked in closed rank with Avery in the middle through the center of the city. Avery wasn't sure where they were headed, but he figured the general would tell him in due time. Ahead of them was a huge brick building situated on the corner of two main roads. There seemed to be a lot of commotion centered there.

"This is Mansion House Union Military Hospital, Avery." Avery could tell that it wasn't built to be a hospital and wondered what it was before the army came. *Someone's fine mansion*, he supposed.

The general and Avery went inside, where the officer had a word with a busy, young, freed man who nodded and walked with them down the corridor and around the corner; Gunner followed close at their heels. A collection of odors assaulted Avery's senses, and he felt both weak and nauseated, but strangely exhilarated, all at the same time. Mechanically he was shaking hands with a doctor, whose name he didn't catch. He stared around him at the beds, cots, and mats. He'd never seen such brokenness. It was like Mrs. Somebody's house, only it was men who were broken. Damaged and bandaged, sleeping or groaning, they were afloat in a sea of misery.

"How do you do?" the doctor was saying. "Mr. Bennett? I say, Mr. Bennett . . ."

"Oh," said Avery, snapping back to the hand he was shaking. "Oh, I'm sorry, sir. I'm Avery Junior Bennett, sir, and I'm afraid I missed your name." Avery was embarrassed with his loss of manners.

The man chuckled. "I can certainly understand that. Quite an overwhelming place, isn't it? My name is Dr. Simpson. I'm the surgeon here at the hospital. I'm in charge of this hospital and a few of the others here in Alexandria. And you're Avery, the grandson of my dear old friend, Clayton Littlefield. Welcome. Your services here will be most appreciated. General Keese has written me about you and has been kind enough to escort you to me. You are highly recommended as being quite knowledgeable, dependable . . . and all the rest. We have young men here who tend to the dressings. Some are medical students and some are volunteers. We need all the help we can get.

"I'd like you to meet Private Matthew Mason, one of our chief corpsmen." Avery shook hands with the pleasant free black man who'd walked them in.

"At the general's request, you'll be boarding with Mrs. Simpson and me in return for your services to the medical corps. I hope that's favorable to you. If so, let us shake on that as gentlemen and get to work."

"Yes, sir, I'll try, I'm . . . well, thank you, sir." They shook hands.

"The general also mentioned you are in search of someone. He thinks this will give you a good opportunity to find the missing person and learn medicine at the same time. Sound good to you?"

Avery smiled. "Yes, sir."

"There's livery in the back of the hospital for your horse and gear. Dr. Mason will show you. It's guarded and your horse will be safe there. Later we'll install you in your room at my place, and your horse can be cared for by my groom, Leon. We'll simply walk to and from the hospitals or use my buggy."

Avery grinned back at the smiling general, and he and Dr. Simpson walked out with him. They shook hands, and Avery thanked him.

"I'll be seeing you around, Private Bennett. Stay safe."

The general waved and rode off with the others.

"Wait! *Private* Bennett?" questioned Avery. "But I'm only fourteen."

Dr. Simpson chuckled. "The rules of war don't permit anyone to fire upon medical personnel. Every doctor, medic, and corpsman treat wounded on both sides equally; both sides need the medical corps, and they agree to treat them as neutrals. This is the safest place for you to be in this war and still be able to complete your family's errand. And this is the perfect place for a young man with an interest in medicine. The general arranged your army commission, *Private* Bennett." He patted Avery's shoulder and moved on down the hallway, chuckling.

"War has rules?" Avery mumbled.

"I'll show you around and show you what your work will be." Dr. Mason, who Avery guessed wasn't much older than him, wore a shirt with the yellow medical corps insignia. His coffee brown face was friendly and outgoing. He walked Avery through the maze that was the Mansion House Army Hospital.

"When we're not working, you can call me Matt."

Avery smiled and nodded at him. It felt like he had a friend. "When we're working, it has to be *Doctor* or *Private*."

"We have a lot of staff and volunteers coming and going here," Matt said. "We have volunteers who come from all over. Several don't serve as soldiers due to their religious convictions, like Jakob Mueller over there; they volunteer to serve their country working here. Some of them have come far distances; some are local people helping out. That tall fellow over there with the water pitchers is Rabbit. He's local, and he's here every day. Some say he's a fugitive slave, but no one's asking him. Then we have orderlies who are paid staff. The orderlies move patients, carry them, and bury them. They are generally strong men who do a lot of our muscle work. Then we have doctors, like you and me, who've some medical knowledge or skills. Some of us are medical school students whose schools have closed for the war. We supervise the volunteers and orderlies. The surgeons are degreed doctors and are in charge of the hospital and all of us. It can get confusing; but don't worry, you'll sort it out."

"Thank you, Doctor," smiled Avery. His head was swimming; and he hoped Dr. Mason was right, that he would sort it out. "I'm not sure I'm really a doctor though."

The corpsman smiled. "You're modest, Dr. Bennett. Your reputation for doctoring the regiments has preceded you. You've had as much experience as most of us here. I'm sure we're all going to get a lot more experience in the next few months. Welcome." They shook hands again, and the friendship was sealed.

All day Avery, with Gunner at his side, watched and learned, wearing his new shirt with the official yellow insignia of the Medical Corps. It didn't take long before Avery and Gunner were known throughout the hospital.

"Let's have a look at that wound, soldier." He changed bandages, cleaned wounds, and checked for infection.

"How'd you learn to do that, Doc?" The soldiers were amazed that Avery could work on their wounds so painlessly.

"My mother taught me," he answered.

"Is that right? Well how about that. She teached you perty good," a soldier said, admiring his snug and tidy bandage.

He carried a basin of clean water to another bedside where the soldier scratched, itched, and squirmed miserably.

"Let's see if we can't help you get a little more comfortable," he suggested. He stripped the soldier, washed his body, and picked off the bed bugs. He turned his straw mattress and put on a clean blanket. He tossed out the basin full of floating dead bed bugs. He carried urinals and basins. He read the patients newspapers, Psalms, and letters from home. He wrote letters for them. He listened to those who were homesick or angry.

Gunner brought smiles and memories to those who were digging holes of depression.

Mather was a forlorn patient who wouldn't eat or talk and seemed ready and willing to die. After meeting Gunner, Mather told Avery about his own hunting dogs back home, all the while rubbing Gunner's ears and smiling with a faraway look in his eyes.

"Guess that old hound would feel really bad if you didn't

show up, huh, Mather? Maybe you ought to get yourself strong so you could go home, what do you think?" Gunner whined and pawed Mather's leg.

"I reckon you're right, Doc. How about some of that chicken broth? Got any left? I might have some of it today."

Some days Avery shadowed Dr. Simpson. The work was exhausting, but Avery thrived on it. Before long his peers were coming to him for answers and assistance. He and Matt Mason worked well together and learned from each other.

"Young Bennett's got a natural ability for healing," Dr. Simpson told his wife at dinner one evening. "It's no surprise. I knew his mother when she was a girl shadowing her father. He was the best doctor Boston ever had. Did you know that, Avery?"

"Well, sir, I didn't, but Major General Keese may have mentioned that," he answered humbly.

One day after Avery had been there for a few weeks, The Committee of Sanitation sent Dr. Simpson a memo concerning the presence of Gunner in the hospital. They asserted that it wasn't hygienic and demanded that the good doctor do something about it immediately.

What he did about it was to speak to Mrs. Simpson. He told her his plan. She sewed a little shoulder cape for Gunner, made from Union uniform material and trimmed out in braid. She sewed the official yellow insignia of the U.S. Army Hospital Medical Corps on each side of the cape.

"Dog's official now," the doctor said. He rubbed his hands together gleefully. Avery had to laugh at the conspiracy, and Gunner seemed quite proud of his little cape.

All the soldiers looked forward to Gunner's visits, and Gunner moved freely around the hospital bringing joy to the sorrowful, laughter and fond memories for the homesick. Avery inquired about Fredric Lennemann from every patient he cared for. No one had come across him.

CHAPTER THIRTEEN

PROMISES KEPT

As autumn winds began to blow and the northern gusts brought heavy frost to tidewater Virginia, the promise of winter close behind, Avery learned from the *Alexandria Gazette* that the Kanawha Valley had convened a Constitutional Convention in October and voted to organize a pro-Union government in Wheeling. They organized a vote to approve secession from Virginia. The new state was, for now, called the State of Kanawha. Avery knew this would be occupying his father's mind. He wondered how he'd voted.

Both armies ceased operations for the winter at the end of November. There would be no new casualties brought in until spring when the skirmishes and the battles would resume. The first winter of the war that saw a nation divided and a state splintered was a bleak and harsh winter. The December wind blew cold and bitter across Virginia.

Dr. Simpson and Avery spent many evenings in the doctor's cozy library in front of the fire. Mrs. Simpson embroidered, while the old and the young doctor discussed the field of medicine. Avery learned a lot from Dr. Simpson, but the old doctor also learned from Avery. Sometimes they spent a pleasant evening reading aloud from the Bible.

One evening Avery told the doctor some ideas he had about reorganizing the wards at the hospital to make it easier for fewer volunteers to give better care. The old doctor had never considered that before and agreed that the hospital was a jumbled maze. He was most impressed with Avery's idea and promised to look into it.

Another evening they discussed Avery's mother's obsession with clean water. The old doctor showed Avery a dusty textbook written by Dr. John Snow. The book, which Avery knew must be very precious, contained two essays, one written in 1849 and the second in 1855. Dr. Snow had studied the cholera outbreak in London in 1849 and was promoting a controversial new theory that the disease was transmitted by water rather than air.

"So this is what my mother was studying?" asked Avery.

"Your mother was a scholar, Avery. I think she got a lot of things right." Avery nodded; he'd always thought that. The young doctor borrowed the book and read it cover to cover. He now understood his mother's insistence on clean water. "She always said it was important. I believe it."

Avery and Gunner continued their rounds every day, getting to know the soldiers and their wives and children in faraway places through letters written and received. And one day, just as Major General Keese had predicted, someone had known Fredric Lennemann. Sergeant Rosman, whose leg was broken and whose body was bruised and scarred, answered Avery.

"Yeah, I knew him. I was a guard at the prison hospital near Manassas last July. He was a wounded prisoner of war. He'd joined up with Porterfield's Confederates. Shot up pretty bad. I helped him write a letter to his wife, but he died before it got sent. Yep, Fredric Lennemann. He's probably buried up in the Confederate Cemetery called Hollywood; it's near Manassas. I've got the letter in my knapsack actually. It never did get sent."

Avery had to sit down on the soldier's bed to take it all in. *Uncle Fredric is dead. Uncle Fredric was a Confederate soldier.* He swallowed and choked. He took some deep breaths and handed Rosman his knapsack.

"What did the letter say? Do you remember?" he asked Sergeant Rosman quietly.

"Yeah, sure, I remember. It was an odd sort of letter; I wouldn't forget that one. Usually when I write for a soldier to his wife, it's all about wondering how she is, how the crops are doing, and how he'll be coming home soon. This letter was all about himself. Then he told me that her family didn't know he was a Southerner and that they wouldn't have guessed he'd joined the Confederacy instead of the Union. So he was running away! Excuse me for saying it, but the man is pig slop, the way I see it." He handed the brown envelope to Avery. It was dirty and bent, but the wax seal was unbroken. "But I promised to deliver his letter."

"I'll deliver the letter for you, Rosman. Thank you very much. My aunt will be indebted to you. Rest that leg now."

Avery felt lightheaded and his heart was aching for Aunt Caroline, who by now probably had a baby to care for; the baby's father was dead. Avery found Dr. Simpson and asked to be excused for the afternoon for personal reasons. He went home to write a letter to Aunt Caroline, but he couldn't think of what to say or how to say it. So, instead, he prayed and wiped away his angry tears. He was too angry and too anguished to be level-headed, that much he knew. He and Gunner took a long walk, and Avery kicked every loose stone that wasn't frozen to the ground.

"It wasn't supposed to be this way, Gunner. We were supposed to bring Uncle Fredric home. Now we'll take this ugly envelope that probably says things that will hurt Aunt Caroline. I don't know what to do. I don't want to go home. But we did find Uncle Fredric—sort of." They stopped walking. "Maybe I won't tell her. We'll just say we couldn't find him." Gunner stood next to Avery and slowly turned around to the direction they'd just come from, and then he sat staring in Avery's eyes.

"You're right, Gunner. You're right. That would be lying. We promised to find him." They walked back to the Simpsons', and Avery wrote a long, sad letter to Aunt Caroline explaining that her husband had been buried in a Confederate cemetery. He told her that the first opportunity he had to do so, he would bring a letter to her, written on Fredric's deathbed.

"This is the hardest letter I ever wrote, Gunner."

A few days later General Keese came to dinner at the Simpsons'. He came to say goodbye for a few months. The army was settled in for the winter at Brandy Station and here at Alexandria, so he was bound for Columbus, Ohio. There he'd regroup and gather some new recruits to train as soldiers. He'd bring them back with him, battle ready, in the spring.

The talk was amiable and cordial, and, although he was sorry to see the general leave, Avery enjoyed the evening's meal of boiled mutton, parsnips, and Harvard pudding. He had mixed emotions, as he realized he would also leave soon, his errand completed.

Suddenly Dr. Simpson asked, "Avery, has Geoffrey told you that he knew your family in Boston?"

"Yes, sir. He mentioned that he did."

"I'll bet he didn't tell you that Caroline was his first love, did he?"

"My dear," interjected Mrs. Simpson, "I hardly think—"

"Oh, poppycock, my dear, I think it's worth mentioning," he cut her off, chuckling.

"I didn't mention it for a lot of reasons," the officer whispered behind his napkin to the doctor.

Avery choked on his cider. When everyone regained his composure, Avery asked, "Will you be taking the train to Parkersburg, general?"

"I will."

"Then you must go the short distance to Kanawha and see them. They would greatly enjoy your visit," pleaded Avery.

"And why don't you come along with me, Avery. Aren't you ready to go home? Your errand is completed; you've located your uncle, and the next few months will be quiet around here; nothing to keep you here."

Avery thought about the little brown envelope he was keeping for Aunt Caroline. He had missed his family.

"Well, yes, sir, I guess. I'd like to go home, and I've thought about it. But I have this job now, and I'd really like to keep it." He realized he sounded presumptuous and felt his face redden; his ears tingled.

"Avery, I've been meaning to talk to you about that very

thing," said the doctor. Avery saw him look at the general and wink.

"Perhaps this is a good time to talk about this. Mrs. Simpson and I feel very blessed to have had you with us for these months. Your presence at the hospital with Gunner has been wonderful for everyone. You have a gift for healing, and I think that you must believe, as I do, that you've a calling in the field of medicine. Your grandfather was a good friend and colleague for many years. Mrs. Simpson and I would like to procure a place at the Medical College of Virginia, in Richmond, for you. It's a very fine institution and one your grandfather would approve. Why you could pass the entrance requirements right now with flying colors. You're one of the best educated and talented young men I've had the pleasure of mentoring.

"The general and I feel it'd be the right thing for you to take your leave of us now and return home to your family. Travel with the general and take him home with you for a visit." He winked at his wife. "Then in the spring, when he returns here for duty, you can travel back with him, work in the hospital for the summer, when I'm sure we're going to be very busy, as this blasted war will be sure to heat up again. Then in the fall we'll get you placed with the incoming class at the college. The director there is a colleague of mine. What do you say, Avery?"

"I . . . I hardly know what to say . . . I mean, it's a lot to think on; but then, not really. I guess, I mean, I would like to do that, oh yes, sir. But, I'm only fourteen years old . . . well, almost fifteen."

Avery knew he was stumbling over his words and probably wasn't making much sense at all. It was a lot to take in. "I'm deeply grateful of your trust in me, Dr. Simpson."

"Then it's all settled, isn't it?" The two men slapped each other on the back and winked at Mrs. Simpson. Avery smiled, as he realized they'd already worked this out ahead of time.

The next two weeks went by quickly as Avery prepared for his trip home. At Mrs. Simpson's suggestion, he and Gunner made a trip to the saddler, where the saddle maker measured Gunner for his first collar and lead. Gunner wasn't sure what this was all about, but he was certain it wasn't to his liking. He lay down and pouted, refusing to stand and be measured. In a week the leather accoutrements were finished. Avery and Mrs. Simpson thought Gunner looked quite handsome, but Gunner pouted with his ears laid back, his tail between his legs.

"It makes you look more citified," Avery teased. "You'll have to wear it on the train."

Avery made a trip to the camp barber for a long-overdue haircut. This was his first real barber cut. A box arrived from the haberdashery in town containing a jacket, shirt, braces, and a pair of trousers that were long enough to reach to his feet. They looked like they were for a man, but Avery was surprised to find they fit him perfectly. On his feet he wore a new right and left shoe. He packed his carpet bag and carefully placed in it the envelope to be delivered to Aunt Caroline. He stared at it momentarily, knowing the sadness it was bringing her. Mrs. Simpson insisted he take an overcoat and a winter hat that Dr. Simpson had long ago grown out of.

"He wasn't always as pudgy as he is now," she noted, "and a trip in this weather will be bitter. You will need it."

"Well," Avery said to Gunner, "I may have left home a boy, but I'm going home looking like a man." The next week General Keese booked the train tickets, including a stable car for their horses.

Avery said goodbye to the doctor and Mrs. Simpson until the spring, promising to return.

He headed off to the depot, arriving early enough to check on Fan's accommodation, which he found satisfactory. She went into a stable car next to the general's gray mule, Smoke. Avery whistled for Gunner, who surprised him by jumping into the stable car. Gunner turned around three times next to the horse and lay down in the fresh straw.

"Looks like you've got your accommodations picked out," laughed Avery.

He walked to the depot where the officer was waiting for

him; they boarded the train. Avery felt a little shiver of excitement as the train whistle blew and the wheels began to screech, rolling westward to a new state now known as West Virginia. He was on his way home.

CHAPTER FOURTEEN

BLIZZARD

When they left Alexandria, the strong, cold wind was blowing heavy snowflakes horizontally through the air. The snow was beginning to pile up along the buildings and the fences. Soon the snow would cover the ground.

Avery watched the winter landscape slip past the train window. The farther they traveled, the deeper the snow became. The train had a snow plow attached to the cow catcher, but periodically they needed to stop to clear off the snow plow and the tracks. At times the blizzard was too heavy to see beyond the window.

The passengers, mostly men, many soldiers, were given blankets and foot warmers, but the air was so chilled that their foot warmers were the only warm things on the train. Many of the soldiers bore the scars of battle and were in various stages of rehabilitation. Avery noted sadly that many had no feet to keep warm. One of the box cars was stacked with frozen bodies wrapped and tied in tarpaulins—soldiers going home.

When the train finally reached Grafton, the station was practically deserted. They were accosted by a woman selling a chicken in a crate. General Keese, finding the promise of fresh meat too tempting to turn down, paid the woman more than a fair price for the chicken. Avery took Gunner out for a quick run. Gunner struggled through the deep snow and was anxious to get back into the stable car. The general threw blankets over the backs of the horses and Gunner; he and Avery boarded the train for Parkersburg.

For two days they watched the snow flying past the window, and soon the snowflakes were synchronized with the rumble of the wheels on the rail; Avery nodded off.

"Parrrkerrrsssburggg!" droned the conductor. Avery awakened with a start. The general was already up and gathering his belongings. Avery looked out the window. The blizzard was worse than ever. With their heads down, they pushed into the wind, catching their breath only by turning around. They made their way to the stable car. They saddled the horse and the mule and gathered their gear. Gunner stood in the door of the stable car looking out at the snowy wilderness, whining, and begging to stay put.

Shouting over the wind in order to be heard, the general yelled to Avery, "Go to the far side of the depot, out of the wind." Avery clung to Fan's bridle and whistled to the reluctant Gunner.

On the far side of the depot, they were out of the wind, but the snow continued to whirl around them. The general was blowing into his gloves. "I think we should find a place to stay here in Parkersburg. This blizzard isn't safe for man or beast."

Avery had been looking forward to being home today, but he understood what the general was saying, and he nodded in agreement.

"AA-frey! AA-frey!" A loud booming voice was calling his name. Avery looked up and coming through the cold and confused passengers was a huge bear of a man.

"Mr. Trotsky! Here I am!" called Avery through the wind.

"Mr. Trotsky, this is Major General Geoffrey Keese. We're traveling together, and he's coming for a visit. General, this is Mr. Trotsky, one of our neighbors," Avery shouted over the wind. Mr. Trotsky nearly lifted the general off his feet, his handshake was so strong.

Mr. Trotsky was almost seven feet tall. He had a huge chest and forearms and was the strongest man Avery had ever known. He looked like the bear whose coat he was wearing. His bear skin coat hung down to his fur lined boots, and he wore a round bear skin hat to match. Even his black wooly beard looked like bear skin. He was a loud, jovial man, but this afternoon, he was all seriousness.

"Zis vetter iss bad businezz. Ve must hurry. Bring your tings. Ze sledge, it is ze onliest good ting today. Come vis me now. Sun and Moon, zey vill get us home."

Sun and Moon were Mr. Trotsky's oxen. He told everyone that their names were Sun and Moon because they worked day and night. The sledge was a large wooden platform used for hauling heavy loads in the snow. Mr. Trotsky stood with the oxen's reins in hand. Lanterns were nailed on the two back corners. Quickly he put their bags and the chicken crate onto the sledge and covered them with bear skins. He picked Gunner up with one hand, put him on the sledge, and covered him with a bear skin. He handed bear skins to Avery and the general, who were mounting their horses.

"You keep your eyes to my lights here and follow," he hollered to them, pointing to the lanterns. He hopped onto the sledge and commanded Sun and Moon to move. Fan and Smoke pushed into the wind. Avery kept his head low behind Fan's neck. "We don't live too awfully far," he called out to the general.

"Good," murmured the muffled response.

Avery thought he'd never been so cold in his life. The general wished he'd followed his better judgment and stayed at the Parker House Inn, instead of following this slow-moving sledge.

Mr. Trotsky sang Hungarian opera at the top of his lungs, while Sun and Moon tramped along through the deep snow. They seemed to know where they were going, even though the road was invisible. Through the long, cold afternoon, the oxen trudged on.

It was almost dark when Avery and General Keese saw lights through the blizzard. Avery pointed, but his chin was so frozen he didn't think he could talk. Sun and Moon jostled a bit as they got out of their rhythm while maneuvering a rather sharp turn. Avery's heart excitedly thumped as he realized the sharp turn meant they'd just turned off the road unto the Bennetts' farm lane. They'd turned into the wind, and the maddening blizzard was now blowing the snow and wind directly into their faces. They could neither talk nor breathe; the cold air filled their lungs, and Mr. Trotsky no longer sang. The light was getting brighter, and they could make out the square shapes of windows; Avery knew he was home. He felt lightheaded and disoriented, and he felt himself slipping from the saddle.

When Avery awoke, it was to the warm smell of food and herbs. The heat from the fireplace burned his face. His legs felt heavy, and he didn't think he could move them. Were they frozen? He opened his eyes. His mother was smiling at him. He could hear the wind whipping around the chimney, and he was glad to be inside, glad to be home.

"Well, I believe the icicle man is thawing out," he heard his mother say. "And how about you, Geoffrey? How are you feeling?" she asked the general.

"I believe we'll both live," he heard the general answer. Avery raised himself onto his elbows and looked around. He and the general were lying on cots layered in quilts in front of the fireplace. Avery could see now why his legs felt so heavy. Gunner was sound asleep across his legs, enjoying the fire, tucked under a quilt.

"Let's warm the innards as well," said Aunt Caroline handing Avery a mug of hot broth. "And one for you as well, Geoffrey." She smiled.

Avery looked around the cheerful, familiar room. His eyes fell on the gun rack. The top row of pegs held his father's Kentucky rifle. Clayton's musket lay across the middle pegs. His own musket rested across the bottom row.

"We're all at home."

"Yes, Avery, thanks be to God, we're all home. Your father and Clayton are both in the barn looking after Fan and Geoffrey's mule and that pitiful frozen chicken you brought home," she said laughing.

"How long have we been here?" asked the general, feeling a bit embarrassed.

"Not too long, maybe an hour or so is all. I think you just made it home in time; you were both about as cold as one can be and still recover."

The general tentatively wiggled his fingers and toes.

"What about Mr. Trotsky? Is he okay?" asked Avery.

"He is. He downed some hot broth and warmed up a bit and went on home to Sofia. He's got a lot to keep him warm!" laughed his mother. "It was so kind of him to go for you, though I'm not sure that it was the wisest decision."

"What time is it?" asked Avery.

"Just about suppertime," answered his mother. "It's been dark for so long today in this blizzard, I think we've all lost track of the time."

Avery looked at the windows nearly covered with snow.

His father and Clayton came stamping into the house, brushing the snow off their boots and pants.

"The snow is almost up to the barn windows," said Clayton, "five or six feet deep!" Avery, the general, and Gunner all shuddered. Clayton set a pail filled with warm milk on the table.

The two men were delighted to see that the general and Avery were both awake and talking. They came across the room to shake hands and welcome them, thankful they were going to recover from the cold. Avery felt warm all over to see Clayton and his father. The fire snapped and hissed, and a baby's cry filled the warm room.

"Oh," said Avery, "I nearly forgot! Aunt Caroline, I need to meet my little cousin."

"Give us one moment, and we'll be in." Avery looked around at the room where he had grown up and realized that the baby was crying from a new addition built off the back of the house. A new room had been added over the summer for Aunt Caroline.

"Phoebe," she said, "this is your cousin, Avery. This is Mr. . . . oh, I mean, this is *General* Keese. And this, gentlemen, is Phoebe."

Avery stared. The tiny person had piercing blue eyes and hardly any hair at all. She had tiny eyebrows that arched as if she were surprised. Her pointed chin looked elfish. Avery was fascinated. He reached out to touch her hand, which she waved into the air, and she gurgled a little laugh. She smiled at Avery.

"Hello, Phoebe," he said quietly. "When did she birth, Aunt Caroline?"

"August 11."

General Keese stretched his legs and got up from the cot. He went to his bag, opened it up, and took out a silver rattle. Phoebe wrapped her tiny fist around the handle and plunged the cold metal ball into her mouth cooing happily.

"Oh, Geoffrey, how thoughtful of you. I know it'll be her favorite. Thank you," said Caroline.

They removed the cots and set the table for supper. Father gave thanks for the venison stew, the fresh bread, and honey; they all gave thanks for the travelers' safety. Everyone had so many questions and so many stories to share that their supper went late into the night, and baby Phoebe fell asleep across the general's knees. Avery felt dreamy. He didn't want to ruin this pleasant evening, but Aunt Caroline's letter couldn't be put off.

"Aunt Caroline, I have something for you." He took the crumpled letter from his knapsack. She opened the letter and quietly read it. When she looked up at the family, Avery was surprised to see that she wasn't crying.

"Fredric's plans didn't include me," she said. "His plan was to settle things at the plantation, join the army, and never return. And he accomplished it." She took in a deep, brave breath.

"I have no tears left to weep," she explained. "Phoebe must never know of his rejection of her. Her father died before she was born." She got up and walked to the fireplace where she picked up the poker, impaled the letter of betrayal, and held it to the flame. "This is over," she said. "Our lives go on."

Everyone breathed and squirmed. *No wonder Rosman called Fredric pig slop*, Avery thought.

"You know that you are not alone. We are all here with you," the general said.

"Yes, I know."

One by one the family embraced Aunt Caroline, reassuring her. She seemed to Avery to be the bravest of all.

"Thank you, Avery, for your promise, your journey, and returning the letter. I am grateful. Bless all of you." She smiled.

Avery watched his family accepting this tragedy and being strong for Aunt Caroline and silently said a prayer of thanks for them all.

It's so good to be home. It's as if I'd never gone away at all; this is exactly how I always remember my home.

CHAPTER FIFTEEN

REUNION

The next day the snow finally stopped falling though the wind continued to blow cold, and the morning after that the sun rose on a brilliant Christmas Day. Following thankful prayers and a warm breakfast, the Bennetts loaded their sleigh with blankets and good things to share. They packed meat, dumplings, crumb cake, pickled beets, and cider on the floor of the sleigh. They brought some logs for the fire; other families would also bring a few logs to throw on the fire. Phoebe was snug in a lamb's wool bunting made from a fleece from neighbor Stempe's sheep farm. Mother and Aunt Caroline were wrapped in their woolen cloaks and quilts. Father and the general drove the sleigh, and Avery, Clayton, and Gunner rode in the last seat. Father's single draft horse, hitched to the sleigh with harnesses and bells, pranced impatiently, waiting for the command to trot off down the road pulling the sleigh alone in the cold, sunshiny day.

When they arrived at the meeting house, the fire in the fireplace was already roaring, sending friendly smoke signals into the blue sky outside. Candles gleamed in every window, welcoming the neighbors. Many tables had been put together and were groaning under the weight of all the food. In the center of the table, stood a small fir tree with Mrs. Mikesell's Moravian ginger cookies hanging on little ribbons from its branches. Decorated with sugar, they looked like little snowflakes.

Following their usual Sabbath meeting, the gathering

hall was festive for Christmas Day with hymns, riddles, food, and thanksgiving prayers. Men were already reciting their puzzles and riddles to the children, who would spend the better part of the day trying to figure out the answers. There might be prizes for those who could figure them out.

Avery's father gathered some of the children together, and asked them "What is this? Four stiff standers, four dilly danders, two lookers, two crookers, and a wig wag." All day the children guessed. This year Avery would have some jokes, songs, and riddles of his own to share.

Some of the neighbors played musical instruments, and everyone sang along. This was unusual for the Quakers, who didn't sing in their meetings. Mr. Trotsky danced with his plump wife, Sofia. Thick yellow braids coiled around her head; she wore an embroidered apron and bright red leather boots. Laughing and smiling, she tried to teach others the dance steps of a folk dance. Aunt Caroline and the general gave it a try. Neighbors clapped and kept time with tapping feet even if their own practices didn't include dancing. Mr. Kohl, who was a woodworker, brought toy spinning tops for all the children.

"You know, Karl works all year long on these to be sure every child has one," his wife whispered. All the children thanked Mr. Kohl a dozen times for the new toys.

"It's nice to see all your family again, Mrs. McDougal."

"And isn't it good to see you, Master Bennett, looking all fine. But all the McDougals aren't about this grand day. The wee ones were a bit cantankerous this morning and stayed home with their sister. I came to help Mr. McDougal keep a hand on all the rest. Glad tidings to all the Bennetts then." She smiled. "Did I hear you've been away?"

He nodded. He told her where he'd been and where he was going. It was probably easier for him to talk to her than to talk to her forward daughter anyway, but he had to admit, he was disappointed.

The general carried the baby and stayed by Aunt Caroline's side. When neighbors paid Aunt Caroline condolences on the loss of her husband, the general steadied her arm. *What was it Dr. Simpson said? Aunt Caroline was the general's first love?* "We need to learn more about that story, don't we, Gunner?"

Avery and the general recited their poem of *The Picket*, and though mugs of cider were raised and applause was plentiful, Avery knew that many in the room didn't understand the words or the war, at least not completely. At this Christmas celebration in this peaceful valley, the only reminder of the war was the uniform of Major General Geoffrey Keese and Mr. Wyatt's oldest son Elmer on crutches, missing one leg. Avery helped himself to another Moravian ginger cookie and shared it with Gunner.

Loud chattering and confusion at the door, where a gust of cold air erupted, grabbed Avery's attention. In came a cluster of red-haired children, chattering excitedly, eager to join the fun. And there among them, gathering up coats and shawls, caps and bonnets, was their big sister, Claire.

Avery froze. Gunner went immediately to the newcomers, tail wagging.

"Gunner doggy!" squealed Colleen.

He felt the panic rising. "Claire's coming to talk to me. What will I say?" he whispered to no one.

"Good day to you, Avery, and a happy Christmas." Claire's eyes twinkled, and he smiled in spite of himself.

"Uh-huh . . . um . . . glad Christmas to you, Claire," he gulped.

"Isn't this an altogether wonderful day, Avery?" asked Claire, smiling.

"Yes. Yes, it is." Gunner sat in front of Claire and looked up, tail wagging.

"Welcome home, by the way."

PART TWO

CITIES OF WAR

1862

CHAPTER SIXTEEN

SPRING IN KANAWHA

It was still gently snowing on January 1, 1862, and the delicate soft flakes were floating lazily through the wintry air. The trees were still blanketed in snow, and the fence posts were still buried from the blizzard a week ago. On this first day of the year, Avery was celebrating his fifteenth birthday. Last evening his father presented him with a book of poetry by John Greenleaf Whittier, a Quaker abolitionist. He looked forward to evenings by the fireside reading and reciting for little Phoebe following the day's chores. General Keese gave him a leather-bound journal. Avery had created journals for himself over the years, but he'd never had a leather one with bound pages. He would fill the pages with knowledge points, new words, and other things that interested him.

"The general's leaving today. He'll be back in the spring when we'll return to Alexandria with him," Avery told Gunner.

"Morning, Avery. Birthday wishes, brother, and a blessed new year to all!"

"Morning, boys." Their father sat down next to Clayton, and the two of them tugged their boots over heavy woolen stockings and headed to the barn.

"Good morning, gentlemen," said the general when they entered the barn. He was readying his mule, Smoke, for his journey.

"So you'll be leaving us, general?" asked Clayton. He approached the mule and petted her muzzle.

"Well, I believe I've tarried long enough. I really must be on my way. I'd like to be back in Ohio by next week. That'll give me about six weeks to train my new recruits and get them ready for the field. It was my pleasure to accompany young Avery back home from Alexandria."

"It's been a pleasure to meet you. Thank you for looking after my son. Your kindness will be rewarded and is much appreciated by his mother and myself. Clayton, will you tell the others to come out, please?"

"Yes, Father." Clayton jogged to the house, and the two men walked slowly out of the barn into the fresh morning. The gentle snowflakes settled on Smoke's eye lashes and mane frosting her gray with white.

"Geoffrey, it's been wonderful to see you again; it's been many years since our younger days in Boston," said Aunt Caroline, coming toward them, wrapped in her shawl. "Please come see us again," she said earnestly and offered her hand. "And . . . please, stay in touch," she added quietly.

"Of course, I shall," he answered. "I'm glad for the opportunity to rekindle our old friendship. Goodbye, Caroline. Sarah, thank you so much for your wonderful hospitality. There are no finer biscuits in these states. And it's been wonderful to see you again. It was a pleasure to have met you, sir, and thank you for your generous hospitality." He shook hands with Father.

"Goodbye, sir, it's been nice to meet you," Clayton said, saluting him. The general returned his salute.

"You're always welcome. We're all very glad you were here. Be safe," said Sarah.

"Well, Avery?" General Keese stood directly in front of young Avery, offering his hand, when suddenly Avery wrapped him in an embrace that surprised and embarrassed both of them.

"Till spring then?" sputtered the officer. "So long, Gunner," he said. "You keep Avery out of trouble now."

"Yes, sir, until the spring. Goodbye, General Keese. Thank you for everything." How could he ever thank the general enough for his guidance and protection since meeting him on the road last year? The general had befriended him, protected him, introduced him to Dr. Simpson, and directed him toward his calling to medicine. And the general and Dr. Simpson had cooked up the scheme for him to attend medical school. He would be forever grateful. He looked forward to the spring when he and the general would return to Alexandria.

General Keese mounted his mule, reined her around, and trotted up the farm lane back to the post road, back to Parkersburg where he would board a riverboat up the Ohio River to the Union post in Ohio.

They all waved and went back into the house and barn, brushing the snowflakes off their shoulders. Avery gave a whistle for Gunner and went to the barn to begin his morning chores. Winter or not, farm chores were still their masters and their time-keepers. Chores and the seasons were both calendar and clock to keep the lives of the valley farmers organized.

Avery spent this winter day as he'd spent several others: doing chores, reading, and reciting nursery rhymes for his little cousin Phoebe.

"What are you building there, Avery?"

With his tools and boards spread around the kitchen floor, he sawed boards and hammered them together. His mother watched him with her hands on her hips and a puzzled look on her face.

"It's a little surprise for Phoebe." No one could guess what it was going to be. He hung the wooden box he made, suspended by rope from the rafters. With her little quilt tucked in snugly around her, Phoebe sat up in the box, giggled, hiccupped, and dozed off, while Avery sang or recited nursery rhymes. Phoebe had a swing!

Gunner walked under the swing, which just reached his back, and kept the swing moving to entertain Phoebe, scratching his back at the same time.

"Gunner, you always manage to find a job, don't you, dog," Avery laughed.

Avery talked to his mother about her medicines and made

notes in his new leather journal of things to remember, which herb for which ailment. One day he told her about his friend, Mrs. Somebody, who lived alone on her homestead. He told her how burn scars had sealed the old woman's eyelids shut. He described how he'd strung ropes from the house to the privy and the barn, so she could find her way. His mother gave him some more ideas that might help the old woman, and together they made some plans to help her.

One wintry evening by the fireside, Clayton announced his intention to study law. No one was surprised, but everyone, especially his lawyer father, was pleased with that decision. Using his father's old law books, Clayton began the arduous task of learning the law of the land under Father's tutelage. They spent their winter evenings poring over the law books. When the Congress resumed next month in Wheeling, he planned to accompany Father to learn the legislative process firsthand.

"I think you'll make a good lawyer, Clayton." Avery sat cross-legged in front of the fire listening to them.

"Why do you say that?"

"Well, because you're like father. You're a good listener; you're fair and square, and you know right from wrong. Sometimes you chose the right thing even if it's the hard thing. All the boys look up to you, Clayton. Yep, you're just how a lawyer should be."

"Those are kind words, Avery," said his mother. "And I agree with you." She smiled at her boys.

Aunt Caroline spent her winter days and evenings creating a needlework sampler to commemorate Phoebe's birth. On a square of linen, which once was part of her petticoat, she was embroidering Phoebe's complete name in fancy lettering. Her name was *Phoebe Caroline Lennemann*. It would say *11 August 1861* across the middle under Phoebe's name. In the lower left corner, in small letters, would be Aunt Caroline's name, and on the right it would say *Fredric Lennemann d. 1861*.

Aunt Caroline and Mother told them all about the beautiful shower of stars that fell all through the night that Phoebe was born. So Aunt Caroline was filling in the background of her sampler with many little embroidered stars. The sampler would hang on the wall next to Avery's and Clayton's name samplers, an official documentation of their births.

Normally in the wintertime, his mother would be filling her quiet time piecing a quilt using the good parts of their worn out clothing.

"No new quilt this winter, Sarah?" Father asked her.

"My scrap basket is hardly full this winter. All the good parts of our worn out clothing are going instead to the United States Sanitary Commission to be used for bandages in the army hospitals. I'm afraid there won't be a new quilt this winter. But I'll manage to stay busy preparing food, mending clothing, and darning stockings." She also managed the household, looked after sick neighbors, and dispensed her remedies.

Avery could tell that his father was restless to get back to the Congress in Wheeling to work on the Constitution for their new state. The Congress had taken a break in December, but he read his weekly newspaper, prepared his arguments, and listed points to be discussed. He discussed these and debated them with Clayton, who was learning a lot about the law. Avery listened carefully, hoping to learn new things.

Sometimes, just for fun, Father would enter into the kitchen work and offer to peel apples for applesauce or take a turn at the butter churn. Avery noticed how much he liked helping Mother with the washing up after supper, just the two of them, smiling at each other. It was a comforting feeling.

Churning butter was Avery's favorite kitchen chore. He never considered it to be women's work, and in the Bennett's household, everyone took turns at all chores. His mother insisted that everyone needed to know how to look after himself. Their jobs weren't divided by girls and boys, but rather by what needed to be done.

The churn and the dash stood in the corner of the room next to the wood box. He milked Aunt Caroline's little goat, strained the milk several times through cheese cloth, poured it into a jug, covered it, and placed it in the spring house. The next day his mother spooned the cream off the top and put it into a jar. When cream filled the jar, it sat in the churn with a cloth over the top, and in a couple of days the cream became clabber. Then it was time to churn. Avery sloshed the milk up and down with the dasher. It sounded like his boots going through mud, *schlug, schlug, schlug.*

"Hey, Gunner, this sounds like you walking through the marsh, doesn't it? *Schlug, schlug, schlug.*" He gave a demonstration of Gunner walking through the mud with the sound effects to the amusement of the family, who laughed when Gunner laid his chin on the floor and covered his eyes with his paws.

Avery sang a churning rhyme for Phoebe. She clapped her hands, and Gunner tapped his tail in rhythm.

"Come, butter, come;
Come, butter, come;
Phoebe stands at the gate,
Waiting for a butter cake.
Come, butter, come."

Years ago his mother sang this to him, and before that she sang it to Clayton. Avery learned to churn the butter using this rhyme. There could be no stopping once the churning began. If he stopped, the butter might be ruined. It took him almost an hour of constant arm movement then. Now that he was older and stronger, it took about thirty minutes. Singing "Come, Butter, Come," made the process go faster, and it amused Phoebe.

Sundays involved a sleigh ride to the meeting house, quiet prayer time, scripture reading, dinner, and the sharing of a newspaper. All the neighbors came to pray together. It was a time to check on the neighbors, learn who was ill, hear who needed help with chores or meals or who needed prayers or helping hands; it was also a time to share good news.

Such was the winter life of the valley's farmers waiting for the spring thaw, which would melt the peace on these hillsides, sending it trickling down the hills and into the icy cold streams of the Kanawha Valley and across the wide state of Virginia.

CHAPTER SEVENTEEN
COURIER FROM CHARLESTON AND TRAIN TO WHEELING

Spring continued to crowd the winter out of its way. The snowdrops were blooming as well as the hellebores and the witch hazel. Avery and Gunner both seemed to have a bit of spring fever and found more and more reasons to stay outside longer.

One day while Avery was dividing onion sets in the shed and his aunt was hanging the wash outside, a courier arrived by horseback. The courier rode speedily up the lane, kicking up reckless chunks of dirt and mud. Avery ran in to grab his musket just in case this was trouble on horseback. He returned to Aunt Caroline's side before the horse drew to an abrupt halt. Avery made certain that the visitor could see the loaded musket.

"I've a packet for a Mrs. Fredric Lennemann. This the Bennett farm? Do I have the right place?"

"You do. I am Mrs. Lennemann." The courier handed her a sealed, important-looking packet. He asked for a drink for him and his horse and left without further comment. Avery sat on the porch step with her.

"What do you think?" he asked.

"It's from a law office in Charleston, South Carolina." She studied the document. "I can't imagine what this is. I don't know anyone there. Except . . ."

Avery saw her blanch pale for a moment, and then she tore open the packet. Her hands began to shake.

"Avery, fetch your father and Clayton. Please?"

By the time the three returned Caroline had read the document; and though she looked pale, she seemed controlled.

"What is it, Caroline?" asked his father.

"Is everything okay, Aunt Caroline?" questioned Clayton.

"I'm quite sure I don't know. I think I'll need some legal advice," she said. "Let's go to the table and sit with my sister."

They all went inside and Aunt Caroline disclosed the contents of the lawyer's letter, written with a great flourish of the quill and blotted carefully.

White, Sneed, and Percival, Esqs., Legal Counselors

51 Queens Row

Charleston, South Carolina

To the Attention of Mrs. Fredric Lennemann

Bennett Farm

Kanawha, West Virginia

Dear Mrs. Lennemann,

I have been instructed by the late Georg and Birgid Lennemann of River's Bend Plantation, Charleston, South Carolina, to convey to you their Last Will and Testament.

River's Bend Plantation, all furnishings, accoutrements, out buildings, land, slaves, and all properties have been deeded, upon the death of both owners, to their daughter-in-law, Caroline Lennemann, and their only grandchild. As you are the only heirs, this will be an uncontested will. The Lennemanns were both of sound mind and body when they filed this document with our office.

Please present yourself, with legal representation, at the earliest convenience to the office of Asheton Percival, Esq., in order to sign the required deed transfers and file the deeds. I remain at your service,

Asheton Percival, Esq., Legal Counsel
Advisor to River's Bend Plantation Estate and executor
for the estate of the late Georg F. Lennemann and Birgid A.
Lennemann

"Avery," she asked Father, "do you think Clayton could be my legal counsel? I know you can't be spared from the Congress in Wheeling. What do you think?"

"Aunt Caroline," said Clayton, "I'm flattered that you'd ask, but I'm too young to do this. I don't know about any of this."

"Caroline, I think that's an excellent idea. Clayton, you're too modest. Yes, you are young, but you can certainly do this, and I'll help you to learn the fine points of land law for this unique situation. Will you give it a try, son? It'll be excellent experience for you."

"You really think I could? Really, Father? Well, if I could study some . . . sure. I'd be honored, Aunt Caroline."

"Clayton, you're older than me; if I can be a doctor, you can be a lawyer," Avery encouraged. He took Father's atlas off the mantel and looked up Charleston, South Carolina.

The following Sunday Clayton and Aunt Caroline presented the first step of their plan. Clayton stood up.

"I wish to share with my brethren a Psalm that has touched my soul this day. 'Behold, how good and how pleasant it is for brethren to dwell together in unity.' Psalm 133:1. God bless you this day." He nodded to a few of the men and sat down. His mother smiled at him from under her bonnet across the room. Several of the meditating men murmured their assent to the Psalm.

After a few moments more of silence, his mother stood up. "Good morning, brothers and sisters. I also wish to share with brethren and pray God's blessings on our assembly. The Lord speaks to me this morning saying, 'Love ye therefore the stranger: for ye were strangers in the land of Egypt.' Deuteronomy 10:19. I discern only one reason why the Lord God would choose to bless us so in this valley; it must be that we must share our milk and honey with those strangers who need to find us. God bless you this day." She sat down and heads bobbed up and down in agreement with her.

Aunt Caroline waited until one of the elders finished speaking, and then she stood up. "My dear peaceable neighbors, I pray God will speak to your hearts this morning. I am meditating this morning on Proverbs 10:12. 'Hatred stirreth up strifes: but love covereth all sins.' Most of you know that I was married to a man who died in the war, the father of my dear Phoebe."

A few bonnets nodded, and Molly McDougal crossed herself.

"His name was Fredric Lennemann. What you don't know is that he died in the service of the Confederacy."

A little rustle of discomfort and surprise passed through the room like a flutter of dove's wings. Avery watched the expressions on the faces of his neighbors.

"I, too, was surprised to learn this. I've received a letter from a legal office in Charleston, South Carolina, apprising me that my daughter and I are the sole heirs of the River's Bend Plantation in Charleston, South Carolina. I've never been there before, but my understanding is that it's a large rice plantation, perhaps the largest one in the entire country. My husband's parents bequeathed this to their daughter-in-law, me, and their only grandchild, Phoebe."

She paused and surveyed the room, trying to read the expressions on the faces of her neighbors. Some of the elders stroked their chins and scowled. They weren't accustomed to hearing the details of the private business matters of neighbors. Many had their heads bowed, but a few looked at her. She cleared her throat, swallowed hard, and continued. A few feet shuffled and a few eyes cast uncomfortable glances about the room.

"I don't have any interest in holding this property. I never met my in-laws; I've never been to South Carolina, and I know nothing of rice cultivation." She paused. "My only interest is in freeing the large number of slaves that reside on that property." All eyes were on Aunt Caroline, and she was aware of the silence.

Avery breathed deeply. He was proud of Aunt Caroline.

"My intentions are to travel to Charleston, in the company of my nephew, who has agreed to be my legal representative. I'll free each of the slaves from all obligations and offer them parcels of the land that they've worked and deeds, if they wish to stay. If they wish to leave, they're free to go. Whatever is left of the holding, I'll offer for sale."

Murmuring filled the room, and heads nodded in approval.

"God bless you, Sister Lennemann," one man said.

"Honorable," said another.

But everyone waited; they knew there must be more to this story, which they presumed would somehow personally involve them. If not, why would she have told them any of this?

"If any of the freedmen have an interest in coming to Kanawha to find a place to live and work, I wonder if any of you would have need to hire any hands? The list of property shows that there are among them blacksmiths, metalworkers, planters, field hands, woodworkers, weavers, carpenters, and household help. Until they are able to find permanent housing, I hope some of you have a spare loft in the barn or an empty shed that might be offered as shelter to these refugees. Please think about this; pray about it and see if you can make room in your hearts and on your farms to feed and shelter any homeless freedmen. Remember that the Lord God has spoken that when we feed and shelter the least among us, we serve Him best. They'll be immigrants who come with nothing. And please also pray for Clayton and myself, as we'll be traveling in enemy territory. Thank you, and God bless you this day."

She sat down as her knees began to tremble. Everyone began talking at once.

"Dear Caroline, you can't be serious about going to Charleston, South Carolina."

"There's a war raging. Have you forgotten that, woman?"

"Caroline, what you do is noble enough, but it's extremely dangerous."

"Please rethink this, Caroline."

"Wait until the war is over, Widow Lennemann."

Aunt Caroline was relieved that their biggest concern was for her and Clayton's safety. No one had expressed concern about bringing the refugees, former slaves, to Kanawha Valley. As the room quieted down, shy Sam McDougal in the back row of men stood up with his hat in his hand.

"Ahem," he began, clearing his voice. His wife gave him an astonished look. "All of you are my good neighbors. You have accepted my family here and allowed us to worship amongst you as other neighbors do. It seems to me that God smiles down on all of us here because of the charity that flows from our valley. It is godly, is it not? And so I stand here to say to you, that I have only a wee barn, as we don't do so much animal husbandry but mostly growin' at our place. And I've a mind that a man shouldn't be livin' in a barn anyway, but in his own place. I don't have the barn you've asked for, but I've land. And if there's men of a mind to give me a hand with it, I think we could put on it a fair cabin or two for the stranger who needs to live and work among us. That's all I got to offer by way of thanks to our Lord in Heaven." He sat down, blushing red. The neighbors stared silently.

Avery was so proud of his aunt, he wanted to hug her. He saw Clayton wink at her and knew that his brother was also proud of her. It's not always easy to choose to do the right thing when it's the hard thing; his father had talked to him and Clayton about this. Clayton had made the hard choice when he left to join the army. Their father had respected his choice, even though he didn't agree. A man or a woman must make those hard choices for themselves, he told the boys. Avery was working this out in his head and understanding it better. His aunt had chosen the hard thing, and Sam's generosity came from his heart. Avery hoped he would always choose the right thing, even if it was the hard thing. Everyone was cooperating with Aunt Caroline's plan, but no one was happy about it, least of all her brother-in-law and her sister.

"You are traveling straight into the battlefield, dear Caroline," they warned her.

"God will be with us. 'Yea, though I walk through the shadow of the valley of death, I will fear no evil,' " she recited.

Father and Clayton would leave for Wheeling the next day. Clayton would return in two weeks to travel with Aunt Caroline to South Carolina.

Clayton and his father had their trunks aboard the wagon, and the draft horse was hitched and waiting when they heard Mr. Trotsky singing as he came walking up the road. Mr. Trotsky would drive them to Parkersburg, where he'd pick up grain and other supplies and then return with the Bennetts' wagon and horse. Clayton and his father would board the train in Parkersburg to travel on to Wheeling. Clayton would spend his travel time studying.

"You already know more than half of the addle-brained lawyers I've dealt with," his father assured him.

"Father, I'm a little concerned about Aunt Caroline's plan to bring the people to Kanawha. What do the delegates say about these matters?" he asked.

"For some reason, that I can't quite grasp, the issue of slavery seems to have a peculiar effect on men who in other ways seem quite sane and sensible. I don't know, Clayton, I really don't know. I am concerned for Caroline and you. I pray about it, and you should join me in that, son. What Caroline is doing isn't just noble, as some said, but it's right. And I have to believe that right will prevail. When we can't believe that, we can't be lawyers."

The two lawyers, former and future, checked into the Wheeling Four Corners Inn and prepared to stay awhile. The Inn was full of delegates, pipe and cigar smoke, loud voices, and the smell of whiskey. Clayton felt awkward in his new suit. A suit was something he hadn't much experience wearing. He was notably the youngest in attendance at this convention of portly, ruddy-faced men, many with full beards or mutton chops.

When Clayton last visited Wheeling, it was a town where folks bought or traded for building materials, farm supplies, and special treats. It was a trip to be taken a couple times of year to visit markets, buy animals, wool, and muslin. Staples for their home like flour, molasses, and sugar came from the general store in Wheeling. Now Wheeling was teeming with important-looking people rather than farm families. Most of the storefronts were glass and the sidewalks were plank. Men in suits were gathered in knots in front of the hotels arguing and debating. Was this the same Wheeling he remembered?

"War seems to change a lot of things," he said to his father.

"It does indeed, Clayton, a lot of things, for better or for worse."

Before falling asleep on the most uncomfortable bed of ropes he'd ever slept on, Clayton said prayers for his father, the delegates' wisdom, and Aunt Caroline's plan. And he dreamed of his cozy loft bed of straw next to Avery.

CHAPTER EIGHTEEN

NOT FROM HERE

While Aunt Caroline and Clayton were in Charleston, Mother had a visitor. Phoebe was napping, and Avery, having finished his chores, had gone up to his loft to read. He planned to have something to eat later and then go hunting with Gunner. He heard his mother opening the door.

"Emma, why Emma Daley, this is a lovely surprise. Do come in. It's a pretty day, isn't it?"

"Spring is in the air, Sarah," said Mrs. Daley. He heard his mother preparing tea while the two ladies chatted, covering most subjects known to the farmers in the Kanawha Valley. When the tea was served, Mrs. Daley's tone changed.

"Do I understand that Caroline's bringing some slaves to our community?"

"Not slaves, Emma—freedmen."

"But why here? Why would she want to bring them here?"

"Why *not* here? We've lots of land, plenty of work, and we're a peaceable and tolerant lot of people. Why not here?"

"Well, I just mean, won't they feel uncomfortable or out of place?"

"I think it will be up to us to make sure they *do* feel comfortable and welcome, don't you?"

Avery heard the hard edge coming on to his mother's tone. *This might get good. No one ever wins an argument with Mother.*

"Well," said Emma, thoughtfully, "I suppose we could make them a church of their own. I mean, they wouldn't want to go to *our* church; they should have *their* church, you know."

"Our church? *Our* church? Whose church is that? Your church? My church? Whose church? Listen to yourself. It's God's meeting place. We're all just refugees here. Why do you think Caroline's newcomers wouldn't feel welcome among us? Whose discomfort are you really concerned about? Perhaps you should ask yourself."

Emma Daley sniffed.

Avery smiled. He lay back in his straw loft with his hands behind his head to listen. *This is when Father would say Mother is getting her English up. Father would enjoy listening to this too.* He knew he shouldn't be eavesdropping, but he was enjoying it.

"Well, Sarah, I just meant . . . you know . . . they're different. *You* know what I mean."

"I don't think I do. That's what you used to say about me when you first met me. You said we were different. And we are. Have you ever known an African person?"

"Well, my goodness, no. I mean, why on earth would I—"

"Well, I have," Sarah interrupted sharply. "Let me educate you. They have two ears, two eyes, two hands, two legs; and they've been endowed by the Creator with a heart, a soul, and a spirit. Does that sound like anyone you know?"

"Oh! I just meant . . . it's just that . . . well you know . . . it's their *color,*" she whispered.

"Their color?" Sarah was incredulous. Avery began to feel tense. *What if others in the valley feel this way?*

"Are you presuming to judge God's creations by their color? Then where would you like to draw the line on acceptable skin color? What is too dark or too light, Emma? Well?"

Avery could tell his mother was struggling to keep control. *Perhaps, I've inherited my temper from Mother. I'll ask Father about that sometime.* He wondered what he would say if someone like Mrs. Daley were speaking to him. Would he be as forthright as his mother?

"Sarah, I'm sorry, I didn't mean to . . . oh dear, what have I said?" mumbled befuddled Mrs. Daley. "I'm just not sure that they . . . that is the sla— . . . the former slaves, I'm just not sure they really belong here in our community. I was just suggesting that they might be happier somewhere else; and perhaps, in our charity, we could find them a better place to go. That's all I was saying. They're . . . you know. They're different," she said in a whispered voice. "They're Africans."

Avery heard the slam on the table, and he knew the family Bible was now sitting in front of Emma Daley. *Mother always provides reference material for settling arguments.*

"Look it up, Emma. Show me where the standard is. While you're at it, find me the description of the neighbors God says we must love. We wouldn't want to love the *wrong* color neighbor now would we?"

"Well . . . I mean . . . it's not *just* color, you know. We don't really know them. What if they . . . you know . . . do things differently or something. And I've heard they don't even speak our language."

His mother said nothing, and without looking Avery knew she was standing with her arms crossed waiting for Mrs. Daley to open the Bible. He imagined that her toe was tapping impatiently. He'd seen this before. He was startled to discover that his own arms were crossed and his body was rigid. *Mrs. Daley is a fine Christian lady. How can she believe these things?*

"The Bible doesn't say we have to harbor thieves and such," Emma said defensively.

"Thieves? Think about what you're saying. You don't know them. None of us do. We don't ever know a new neighbor, do we? Did we know you and Mr. Daley when you moved here from Chicago? Did anyone suggest that since you came from a big city that you might not be comfortable here? Did anyone suggest that you were anything other than good?" She let Emma think about that a minute.

"Remember, how you were once suspicious of us neighbors from the East? Remember all the notions you had about us

Quakers? And here you are having tea with me."

"Well, no, but . . . but that was different."

"How? How is it different? Better look up what Scripture says about welcoming the stranger. Weren't we Friends kind to you, even though we didn't know you? I must say, I'm quite surprised at you. These are meek and downtrodden people who need us. I'm disappointed in your Christian thinking."

By now Emma Daley was sobbing and blowing her nose. "Sarah, I . . . I don't know what to say . . . I . . . I'm so sorry, but I can't help it. Of course I want to be charitable, but this is so different. And, well . . . I'm afraid of them. You're right, of course. I am judging people that I don't know. But how do I know that I *want* to know them? I don't mean to be a bad person, I'm only trying to protect our community."

"What do we need to be protected from? That's God's job, isn't it?"

"Sarah, are you saying you aren't concerned about them?"

"I'm concerned that wrong-thinking people like you will make their life here more difficult than it needs to be. But, no, I think if city people like you and I can come here to the wilderness and learn to make a good life, and if we all can feel welcome in this valley and pray together, then anyone could, regardless of their color."

"Well." She sniffed and blew her nose. "Well, I hope you're right. I certainly don't wish this to come between us or our friendship."

"It needn't," Sarah answered abruptly.

"Well, if you're feeling self-righteous, you must think me a bad person."

"Emma, I never thought that for a moment. You're a good person with some wrong thoughts."

"Perhaps you're right. I'll try to rethink this. And I'll think about what you said. I am feeling confused about it all right now, and I'm just afraid. It's all new, you know. I'm sorry."

"If you're sorry, you need to take that up with God. You owe me no apology. I'm happy if your thinking has changed this day. If your thinking hasn't changed, I'll pray that it will. As for me, this conversation will never be mentioned again. It's behind us. Let me hot up your tea; it's certainly gone cold on you. Are you planning to divide any of your four o'clocks this spring? If you do, I'd love to have some. I need some bright flowers by the new room addition we built on for Caroline." Avery could tell by the tone of his mother's voice that the discussion was over and would never be mentioned again.

"Oh yes, I will be dividing my flowers, and I'd love to bring you some; I know you've admired them. They do add some lovely color."

Avery was ready for Mrs. Daley to leave so he could get out of the loft, go to the privy, and then go hunting, but he didn't want either woman to know that he'd heard this conversation. He was proud of his mother, but he knew she wouldn't be pleased that he'd listened, so he wouldn't mention it.

He'd be gone to Alexandria before Aunt Caroline's refugees arrived. He was sorry he'd miss that. He prayed that no one else would be wrong-minded like Mrs. Daley. *But if they are, my mother will sure fix that!*

Avery tried to gather his thoughts and began to gather his gear a little each day. As the spring days were winning the weather battle, he was sure that General Keese would soon be arriving. And he was right. It was on a warm day with a strong breeze carrying the promise of spring. The daffodils were blooming; and some of the fruit trees were budding, laughing at winter, while risking all.

The general tarried but two days, visiting and playing with Phoebe and the new rag doll he brought to her, and taking quiet walks with Aunt Caroline. He gave them chilling news of the war and dreadful battles to the west; apparently not all the armies had taken the winter off.

Three days later, with panniers packed, Avery and the general rode down the lane on Fan and Smoke with Gunner at their heels. They'd be going to Parkersburg to take the train to Grafton. It was good to see his friend again, and he was eager to return to the hospital and his job.

At the Grafton train depot, General Keese met up with his new recruits from Ohio. As they were preparing to board the train for the last leg of the journey, Avery told him that he would meet him back in Alexandria. He needed to make a stop along the way. The general wasn't pleased with this news.

"Avery, the turnpike isn't going to be as safe as it was a year ago. The Confederacy has dug in pretty well. You could encounter battles—or worse. This isn't a good decision. I'd like to change your mind."

"Well, sir, it's kind of a life-or-death situation. It's an important errand. I'll be fine, and I'll only be a week behind you."

"Your mother would have my stripes for this, Avery."

Avery laughed at the general's joke. "If it's my mother your worried about, sir, you'd better worry about more than just your stripes." They both laughed and shook hands.

"Avery, I mean it. Be careful, be alert, and be ready. God keep you. I'll see you in a few weeks in Alexandria. A man must do what he feels called to do."

CHAPTER NINETEEN

A NEW VISION

Avery's trip this time would be much faster with Fan's help. They trotted off toward the turnpike. After only three days riding, he spotted the silhouettes of the familiar farm buildings. His heart pumped a little extra, and his stomach was turning. What would he find when he got there? Would she have managed on her own? Would she still be alive? He had prayed daily for Mrs. Somebody since leaving her last summer. He'd promised himself he'd return when the war was over, but he couldn't wait that long.

"Okay, Gunner, let's check it out." They trotted the rest of the way to the farm. As they approached, Avery noticed the ropes he'd used to line the paths for her were still in place. He hoped she'd used them to find her way around her farm. It looked like a spider web from the turnpike. Everything looked quiet. He slid off Fan and walked to the porch, afraid of what he'd find.

"Rose? Mrs. Somebody? It's me, Avery." Gunner went sniffing at the door and pawed it until it cracked open. The nose went in first, and then the rest of him bolted inside. The door shut slightly behind him, catching his tail, and he jumped forward.

"Hey," her voice cackled, "that you, boy? Hey, would this be Gunner?" The dog was dancing around her, tail wagging, happy to see the old woman.

Avery laughed. "Looks like Gunner was as worried about you as I was."

"Well, I jus' knowed I was havin' me a good day t'day," she exclaimed.

"Mrs. Somebody, how are you? Are you doing okay? Do you have food? Are you well?"

"Well, mercy, boy, you are feelin' right nosy t'day, ain't ya, ol' Mr. Nosy Avery Junior Bennett?"

"I'm sorry, I didn't mean to be, it's just . . . well, it's good to see you, and it looks like you're well, and I guess I'm just excited. It's good to see you, Rose."

"Ah ha," she slapped her leg, "you 'member mah name be Rose!"

"I'll never forget. How are your eyes, Rose?"

"Well, sir, I soaked 'em a lot, like ya tol' me ta do, and I got me some little slits here to look out. An I can see you a little bit."

"Rose, that's great news. I brought some things to fix your eyes. It won't be nice, and you'll be uncomfortable for a few days; but in the end, your eyes will be open and you should see. Do you want to try that?"

"Well, let's git on with it then. In case you didn't notice, the chariot didn't come yet." She plopped herself down on her cot.

"This where ya want me, Dr. Avery Junior Bennett?"

Avery had talked to his mother about the scars that grew across Rose's eyelids preventing them from opening. They devised a procedure that they both thought might work. Using his grandfather's scalpel, he'd practiced at home making the smallest, lightest incisions, until he could split the skin of an apple without ever touching the apple. He practiced on leather, vegetables, and paper. At home he felt so confident. Now looking at the fragile old woman lying on the cot, he swallowed hard and prayed.

"I'm going to wash your face first, Rose, with warm soap and water. Then I'm going to tie your hands down."

"Why you need to do that? I don't like that."

"I know, Rose, and I don't like doing it. It's just so that you don't accidentally hit my hand and cause me to cut your eye. We can't take any chances," he explained. This was his mother's idea. He tied her hands firmly at her sides.

"I don't like this, you know," she pouted.

"Yes, I know."

He washed his own hands with lots of soap. Then he opened the kit his mother had put together and laid everything out on a clean piece of linen. The scalpel, a few other instruments, and a magnifying glass were all wrapped in the flannel packet his mother sent. These all belonged to his grandfather, the skilled surgeon from Boston.

The water was warm. "Okay, Rose, I'm going to wash your face with warm water and lots of soap."

"Well, okay. Looks like you the boss man, Mr. Fourteen-Years-Old Surgeon Boy."

"I'm fifteen now, Rose."

"Oh, well then, all growed are you?"

"Not yet, still growing." He chatted to relieve his nervousness and to reassure Rose.

"Well, next time yer come yer better duck down yer head; yer cain't hardly fit under the door now, cain't yer? Yer like to fill up this here room." This nervous conversation continued, while Avery washed, soaped, rinsed, and dried the scarred and shiny old face. When he was satisfied, he took out a little green, glass bottle with a glass stopper and poured some of the liquid onto a stack of clean linen squares.

"Rose, I'm going to put some cloths by your mouth and nose, and I want you to take a deep breath in." He hoped he didn't sound as nervous as he was. He held the stack over Rose's nose and mouth, and she breathed in deeply. He removed them, and she said, "Okay, now what?" He was very surprised. He expected her to go right to sleep. So they did it again, and she said, "Oka-a-ay, now-w-w wh . . .," and she dropped off to sleep.

Avery moved quickly. His mother warned that she wouldn't stay asleep long. He put the magnifying glass close to her eyelid and took a good look at how the scarring lay. He pulled up on the eyelid; he could see the edges of the scar tissue. Carefully, with his grandfather's scalpel, he lightly released the scar tissue from side to side. He pulled up on the eyelid, and it was completely open. He breathed and said a grateful prayer while beginning the second eye, repeating all the steps. Just as he finished, Rose began mumbling and tried to lift her arms. He quickly washed up and put everything away. He'd clean and boil them all later. When she stirred again, she opened her eyes. Avery saw that they were light gray in color. The few eyelashes were gray and singed unevenly.

"Ah sees," she announced bravely. "Ah sees!" She nearly shouted with glee. "And ain't yer the handsomest cuss I ever did see!" She laughed and tried to sit up.

"Don't sit up quite yet, Rose," He laid her back down and untied her hands.

"Why not? I gots to go try out my eyes. There's some things I got to see to," she said sounding like her old self. "Heh-heh, that's a little joke, ain't it." She was delighted with her play on words.

"Good joke, Rose. Now you just lay still a little while here."

He took out some salve and lightly applied it to the freshly released eyelid. You will need to do this every day for the next weeks, Rose. It's very important. Always wash your hands first, okay?"

"Where you gonna be?" she asked him.

"Rose, I can only stay a day or two. Then I need to get on to Alexandria. I'm in the U.S. Army now, and I have to go, or I might meet the war on the way."

"The war? What war?" she demanded. He reminded her about the Home Guard that had destroyed her place and stolen her very life for what they called the "war effort."

"You mean it really was a war? I thought they was all talk and smoke; didn't know it was a real war."

So while trying to keep her quiet as the chloroform worked itself out of her body, he told her all he knew about the war. She seemed to soak it all in.

"Most of the men folk kin I got all got killed when I's but a small girl. My grandpappy, my pappy, my uncles, cousins, and my onliest brother, they all got kilt in the war to get freedom from the King of England. Seems to me that shoulda been enough men dyin' fer freedom. Now they's some what don't agree about freedom fer ever'body? That what yer tellin' me?"

"Well, sort of, Rose. It's a bit more complicated than that. But, well, maybe that is it. Sorry about your men folk." Avery was doing some mathematical figuring in his head. He was interested in her reference to the Revolutionary War.

"How old are you, Rose?"

"Don't know really." He could tell she was telling him the truth. "I been around a few winters, Avery."

"Do you have an old family Bible?"

"Cain't read, what I need the Bible Book fer?"

"It might tell how old you are." She lay still thinking about it.

"You see that heap o' covers by the chimley?"

"Yes."

"They be's an ol' cradle under it."

Avery went to the chimney corner and lifted up the pile of comforters and old quilts, ragged and mildewed. Beneath the pile in a hollowed out place in the dirt floor was a cradle. He stared in disbelief. How had the marauders missed this? How had he missed it? He'd cleaned up this room and moved around in it for a month or more. How had he never seen this?

"Wondrin' where it's been at?" she asked, reading his thoughts.

Gunner got himself up from his nap, stretched, yawned, and investigated the smells stored in the pile of bedding, reading their history.

"Yes, I was wondering. I didn't see this here before."

"Weren't here when yer was here. I moved it. It's been livin' under my bed here. I pulled it out. Since I could see a little bitty slit, I just wanted to look at it agin."

"It's a beautiful carved cradle. I'm glad the marauders didn't break it up."

"Yeah, me too. But don't go git'n sentimental now. Lift the bottom up out the cradle."

He lifted the entire cradle out of the corner hiding place and put it in the room. Gunner came close. Avery lifted the fitted board which when wrapped in soft cloth would serve as a mattress for the baby. Under the board was a dropped bottom. The secret space held the family Bible, a tiny silver spoon with a rose worked into the handle, and a tiny wooden cross. There was a brooch with a rose cameo instead of a cameo head. *These are all the treasures she has in the entire world.*

"Well, go on there. Have a look," she said. He knelt down and carefully lifted the Bible out. It was very old and fragile, and he held it gently. It had beautifully colored designs inked on some of the pages. The inside covers and the edges of the pages were decorated with bright swirls of colors, like reflections in a trout stream. He opened it to the middle, where he found what he was looking for. It was all there, Rose's family history amidst the beautiful leaves, gold scrolls, and colored designs, unlike anything he'd ever seen. He worked his way through the lineage of names with no faces, until he came to Rose Marie Holtom.

"Are you Rose Marie Holtom?"

"Marie is my mama's name. She's dead and I reckon the name oughter die with her. I'll jus' be Rose Holtom."

Avery thought about that. If his father died, should he give up his name? No, his father had given it to him.

"Don't you think your mother gave you her name so it could live on after she was gone? Don't you think she would be proud to have you carrying her name?"

"I dunno. I didn't think on that. Just didn't want ter claim somethin' that weren't mine," she answered honestly.

"I think your mother would be proud to have you be Rose Marie."

"Ya think that, do ya? What's it say in there, Mr. Fifteen-Years-Old Reader Boy?" she nodded toward the Bible.

"It says that Rose Marie Holtom was born August 15, 1768. Your parents were Wilmer and Marie Holtom. You might be interested to know that Rose was also your grandmother's name."

"Is that right? No one said that. I didn't know that. How

old am I, Reader Boy, can you do sums?"

"You are ninety-four years old, Rose."

She chuckled. "Guess that makes me a Miss Somebody after all."

"I knew it all along."

In a couple of days, it was obvious to Avery that Rose's eyes were going to heal well, and she was caring for them exactly as he taught her. He cut her some wood, checked out her supplies, and found a couple of things needing repair. He gave her some packets of vegetable seeds. He and Gunner went squirrel hunting but came home with a rabbit, which tickled the old lady.

"You might be a smart Reader Boy, but you sure don't know a squirrel from a rabbit," she hooted. He was sure now that she could see that she'd be able to take care of herself. It occurred to him in a humbling moment that she'd taken care of herself for at least eighty years since her mother died, without any help from him.

With everything in order and prayers of gratitude for the successful eye lid surgery—prayers for her safety and his—Avery, Gunner, and Fan headed off to Alexandria.

CHAPTER TWENTY

RETURN TO ALEXANDRIA

He remembered how he felt the first time he'd seen Alexandria. He felt the same thrill now, looking down from the hilltop for the second time.

But the difference between then and now stunned him. This was a city at war. Since leaving Rose's place, he'd seen a lot of smoke along the horizon. Gunner occasionally responded to the sound of distant artillery. They met columns of soldiers along the turnpike. The soldiers were too tired and battered to look deeper into the wooded edge along the roadside to see the travelers. Sometimes he couldn't tell if the column was Union or Confederate; they were that used up.

He wore his official yellow medical corps shirt over his jacket, identifying him as a medical corpsman. General Keese told him to be sure his insignia was visible in case he met up with a soldier itching to shoot somebody. His shirt was visible, but unless he saw someone in need of medical service, he kept himself out of sight. Everyone *should* know that the rules of war say you can't shoot a medical corpsman, but what if someone didn't know or chose to ignore the rules?

Alexandria was the winter quarter of the U.S. Army, the Union forces. The enemy's camp was only one hundred miles away in Richmond. In this heavily wooded, expansive state of Virginia, anyone could really be anywhere. He kept his musket ready at his side, and he was vigilant. Gunner put himself on picket duty and led with his nose, evaluating the recent activity on the trail they were following into town. The city of Alexandria now looked like two cities, it seemed to Avery. The fine houses, churches, and merchant shops that were headquarters, hospitals, and holds for prisoners, he had seen before; and now a second city, made of Sibley tents with Sibley stoves, cooking fires, and exercise grounds, housed thousands of soldiers. Women came and went from the camps. They washed clothes in tubs over the fires, baked their bread, and did the soldiers' mending. Smoke, noise, and confusion enveloped the entire city. Avery wondered if the air was safe to breathe; it choked him. Families loyal to the Union tried to live a normal life in Alexandria, but it was anything but normal under Union occupancy. The city was in chaos. The streets were crowded with disorderly soldiers. Drunken Union soldiers were lying on the sidewalks. He rode cautiously through the town square and up the slight hill on the other side to Dr. Simpson's home. He was already thinking about Mrs. Simpson's apple cobbler. Gunner looked at him and drooled as if reading Avery's thoughts.

Mrs. Simpson was in a jolly mood and ever so happy to see Avery and Gunner.

"When the general told us you'd left him, we were all terribly worried about you. Everyone will be very relieved to see you, young man," said the motherly Mrs. Simpson. "You take your things on up to your room and then put Fan in the livery with Leon while I fix you something to eat." Gunner nuzzled her hand. "And, of course, we worried about you too, Gunner." At supper that night Dr. Simpson filled Avery in on the details of the hospital. The war had indeed heated up again, as the doctor had predicted.

Avery was happy to be back in Alexandria, but his brief rest and social visit with Dr. and Mrs. Simpson ended after breakfast the next morning when he, Gunner, and Dr. Simpson headed out in the doctor's buggy through the turbulent city of Alexandria to the hospital. Unhappy Fan pawed the ground and whinnied. She was comfortable and well fed, but she was unhappy about being left behind in the Simpson's stable.

Avery shadowed Dr. Simpson to learn as much as he

could about all the patients he'd be seeing and their conditions. He could see the ravages of war all around him once more. Some of the patients were outside on the lawn under the large trees, talking and playing cards; some were playing with Gunner, who was back on duty wearing his official cape. Avery tried to speak to all of them, but now there were hundreds who all needed immediate attention.

In addition to the Mansion House Hospital on Fairfax Street, which held five hundred beds, there were other homes and buildings now serving as hospitals. His friend Matthew Mason was the medical corpsman in charge of one of those hospitals under Dr. Simpson. In addition, Alexandria now had five prisons holding Union deserters and Confederate prisoners of war, who also needed medical attention. Having been raised to respect all life, Avery found it difficult to accept the haphazard treatment of human life during the war. Sometimes he just wanted to scream "Stop!" at all the wounding and the killing.

One thing that had improved in the hospitals since the first year of the war was the addition of trained women nurses. They now had a large staff of nurses trained by a woman named Dorthea Dix, who had opened a nurses' training school.

"Their skills are a definite improvement for all of us," Dr. Simpson told him. "There are men who don't believe the women should be here at all, and others who think they'll be in the way, fainting here and there with vapors. They don't give women enough credit," he asserted. "I've yet to see a single one of them faint in this hot stench of unbelievable sights and torture. I'd trade three male nurses for the likes of one of these female nurses." He looked at Avery and his eyes were twinkling. "And for your mother, I'd trade five!"

Avery laughed, but he thought it was probably true.

It looked like a long, hot summer was in store for all the hospitals and the medical personnel in Alexandria. Avery came every morning to Mansion House Hospital with Dr. Simpson, and after midday break he and Gunner headed across town to assist with treatments of wounds in the other hospitals. He looked forward to this, because he usually saw Matt.

Avery's reputation for wound treatment was growing. Experienced surgeons were listening to his treatment regimens, learning from Avery; they were noticing less infection. The days were long and the work was hard. The many trips up and down the three-storied building exhausted Avery and the rest of the staff. Many days he and Dr. Simpson were so tired that as soon as supper was over, they had short conversations and went to bed. Gunner curled at Avery's feet and didn't move until breakfast.

"As daylight comes earlier, we'll have longer daylight hours to perform surgery. Ambulances will be able to bring the patients in earlier. With longer days, they'll get more of them off the battlefield before dark hopefully. Unfortunately for all of us here, it means longer days."

Avery nodded. "Perhaps fewer will die waiting for the morning."

CHAPTER TWENTY-ONE

NEW NEIGHBORS

Sarah had enjoyed her quiet time alone with Phoebe while everyone else was away. She walked her around the gardens, showed her the flowers, and taught her their names. She taught her to "moo" and say "cow." They played peek-a-boo, and Sarah recalled all the rhymes she'd stored in the attic of her memory since her sons were small. She rocked Phoebe in her swing. The little girl learned to pull herself up to stand and then fell down laughing.

"Little Miss Phoebe, before long you'll be ready to learn to read. You know what Aunt Sarah is thinking? I'm thinking that you'll need a school. You and all the children of the hollers and the new children from South Carolina, you will all need a school. What do you think about that? School!"

"Scoo," mimicked Phoebe.

"Yes, Phoebe, school. Kanawha needs to be modern. Let's make a plan."

She sent away to Boston for textbooks and materials. She wrote a letter to the Congress in Wheeling explaining her plan and asking for recommendations and funding. She learned that in Parkersburg last January seven men from the school board started a school for black children. She wrote to them for recommendations. She was grateful that she and Caroline had a substantial inheritance from their parents. She would use some of hers to establish her school.

By the time Aunt Caroline and Clayton returned to Kanawha with their wagonload of four families, little Phoebe had added two teeth to her smile, a ribbon in her fuzzy hair, and several new words, including "school." She had no idea what school meant, but she knew Aunt Sarah was excited by the word. Aunt Caroline and Clayton shared their news of the trip and events at River's Bend Plantation and the horrors of the hungry South.

"Mr. Percival believes it will sell at good price in spite of the war," Clayton explained. "The war could create some problems for Charleston however. Right now there are a lot of people with grand homes full of beautiful furnishings, but no one has any real money or any hope of making any money soon. The economy of Charleston has completely come apart with the loss of their slaves and the loss of thousands of men. Their economy was based entirely on rice, indigo, and cotton. Without the slaves, the rice is doomed, and with the blockade, so are the cotton sales. Charleston seems to be right on the edge of the hardships. Other cities are already disasters. The entire South is hungry and helpless, Mother. We saw some pretty awful things. Perhaps Charleston will miss the worst of it. They can only wait and hope for the best."

Sarah looked with wonderment at her son. Wasn't it only yesterday she was holding his hand through the garden and teaching him the names of Virginia's cities? *What a splendid man he is becoming*, she thought. *He is so like his father; he'll be a brilliant lawyer.*

Later Sarah told them about her plan for the school, which they greeted with enthusiasm.

"Scoo-scoo," screeched Phoebe, clapping her little hands together, knowing that this word somehow generated great excitement.

The four shy families were made as comfortable as possible. Aunt Caroline and Sarah spread quilts and blankets on the clean straw in the barn, and the families all spent the night there. The next day Clayton made visits throughout the hollers to find work for the families, while on the corner of the McDougal's potato farm cottages were being built. Clayton took two days to rest, bathe, wash his clothes, and pack. He went hunting and fishing and brought pheasant and trout home for the women and the newcomers.

"I read in the papers in Charleston that the Congress in Wheeling is arguing the legality of the constitution of West Virginia. I want to hear the arguments, especially Father's," he said as he packed his things. The next day he left for Wheeling to go to Congress, feeling quite experienced and comfortable in his suit.

The two women continued to run the farm and raise Phoebe. Three of the four families found work and housing in one or another of the hollers in Kanawha's fertile valley. The fourth family with their two small children stayed with the Bennetts. The man, known as Banjo, was adept at many things, and the two women felt they could use the extra help. Kanawha neighbors helped Banjo build a house and privy on the Bennett's property.

"The spring crops will soon be coming in, and the hens will be layin' again," Banjo's wife, Maize, said. "I tend chickens; it's my particular thing to do, geese too." Maize could also help with the cooking and household tasks while Sarah and Aunt Caroline taught school. Maize's two children would attend Sarah's school. It was all working out so well; Aunt Caroline and Sarah sighed with relief.

They watched the post road for the arrival of books and materials that Sarah's Boston friends were sending. They wrote long lists of things they hoped to teach the children of the valley. When they had their plans thoroughly in place, they announced it on a Sunday.

Following the announcement, while families were sharing their Sunday dinner, Sarah saw Emma Daley give small fabric bags to Emily-Birgid and Clem, Maize's and Banjo's children. The children smiled and thanked Mrs. Daley. Sarah watched Emily-Birgid pull out a necklace that Mrs. Daley had made for her using the china berries from her china berry tree. She had dried the berries, dyed them with indigo, and strung them on a string. Mrs. Daley helped the pleased child put them over her head. Clem dumped his bag and buckeyes fell out onto the floor and immediately caught the attention of some of the other small boys who used buckeyes for marble games. Sarah wanted to shout with joy. Emma Daley had made a big change in her life. If Emma could do it, then so could others. Sarah couldn't wait to write and tell Avery. *I know he was eavesdropping when Emma Daley came to visit. This will relieve his mind.*

CHAPTER TWENTY-TWO

NURSE IN ALEXANDRIA

One summer afternoon Avery and Gunner were resting in the yard. Avery lay out on the grass following several hours in surgery. He'd barely closed his eyes when he felt a nudge on his leg. Believing it to be Gunner, he reached out with his hand to pet his muzzle, but his hand locked around a soft shoe.

"This how the good doctor spends his time idling?" a soft female voice asked. He sat up and squinted into the sun at the silhouette facing him.

"Hello?" he inquired.

"Well, that's not much of a hello, I'm thinkin'. That the best you can do for a lass that's crossed half the nation to see you now?"

Still blinded by the sun, Avery scrambled to his feet and looked down at a soft, pale face surrounded by a green bonnet. Independent red curls peeked out wherever they escaped.

"Claire? Tater Claire? Wh-why are you here? How . . . how did you get here? Wh-what are you doing here?" he stammered.

"Well, for sure you're askin' a lot of questions; now which one is it you want answered?"

"What are you doing here?" He felt like he must be dreaming this. Was he dreaming of home perhaps?

"I'm reportin' for my duty. I'm a nurse, Avery. I took the studies with the lady Dorthea Dix, and I did real well; at the top of my class, I was. Now I'm comin' here to work and be a help to my country."

"They sent you *here*? A year ago there were only sixteen army hospitals, but now we've got two hundred and four! And you got sent here? Huh."

"I requested to come here to be with you. Now listen here; this is my plan. I want you to hear it straight from me. I'll stay here and work one year. Then you can tell me to stay or go. At the end of one year, if you want to always be by my side, I'll stay on with you, and I'll marry you whenever you want and be at your side forever. If you don't want me, then you say, *Tater go home.* If I'm a bother to you, or you don't want me, then I just go, like that. What do you say about that?"

Avery was dumbfounded. He knew his mouth was hanging open, but nothing was coming out. Finally he choked out some words.

"What? What do I say? Have you lost your wits girl? I'm fifteen years old! I never thought on getting married. I mean, well, probably sometime, but I'm not thinking on it *now.*"

"Well, I'm sixteen, and I did think on it. I know that when you're grown, you'll be the man I want to marry, so I thought we should be straight on that from the start. I won't be saying anything more about it. I'm not your girl; we're not betrothed; nothing like that. I just want to be here and be your friend, and you can get to know me. Maybe you'll decide that I'm the girl you'll want to marry—whenever we're grown and ready, that is. Just wanted you to know what was on my mind, so I've put it to you honest-like. I won't be speaking about it again. I have to get my apron on and get to work now. It's nice to see you again, Avery, and I know we'll enjoy working together." She walked straight into the steaming hospital without ever looking back.

"Huh!" he said to himself, but Gunner was listening, ears cocked. "She's a proud one, isn't she? Imagine that. She chose me! Shoot. She's plenty bossy, that's for sure, huh, Gunner? We'll stay out of her way, that's for sure! Huh. Imagine that. She just planned out my whole life. Who's she think she is?"

He knew his face and ears were red. He hoped no one else had heard that silly girl making her plans for his life. "I should've guessed the day she handed me those violets after I'd saved her sister from drowning that she was up to something. She's forward *and* bossy, Gunner."

Day after day the ambulance wagons came rolling in from the distant field hospitals. As soon as the battle victims were stable enough to travel, they loaded them into the ambulances and began their long journeys to the army hospitals, sometimes by train. Sometimes the wounded were stacked upon wounded.

"Dr. Simpson," called Avery. "Sir, the field hospitals are reckless. They're sending patients before they are stable. They're amputating limbs that might have been saved had they taken more care. Disease is festering in those ambulance wagons," he warned. "Something needs to be done."

Every day Avery worked beside the nurses. Often the nurse beside him was Claire. *Where'd she come from?* Avery wondered. *She seems to know what I need before I even ask. Whenever I need assistance, she appears almost magically. She might be bold and bossy, Gunner, but she's a good nurse, strong, tireless, and knowledgeable, gentle but firm with the patients.* Avery admired her skill and enjoyed working with her, but he would never admit to it. He'd forgiven her, and all but forgotten the speech she'd made.

The Sanitary Commission visited the field hospitals and instructed all the staff in proper camp procedure. They put nurses in place to enforce their instructions on drainage, latrine placement, water supply, and disposal of waste material, such as putrid bandages and amputated limbs with gangrene. All of this helped to reduce the instances of disease and sickness among the Federal troops. But here in the hospitals, the crowded conditions and the infections still took a major toll, and Avery continued to complain.

One evening at supper, tired Dr. Simpson told his wife and Avery that the true tragedy of the war was that more men were dying from dysentery, diarrhea, typhoid, pneumonia, and malaria than from their wounds. He had the actual count in his reports, so he knew this to be true. Avery said he'd suspected as much.

The post office down the street was turned into a hospital, and those raw wooden floors were already saturated with dark blood stains. There were no cots or beds there yet, and the men were treated while lying on the post office floor. And still they kept coming.

"Gunner, I hadn't realized that there were this many men in all of the United States." Avery was exhausted.

He assisted in surgery for hours, made rounds regularly, treated and dressed wounds at several hospitals, and instructed others. Claire emptied urinals, cleaned beds, walked patients, read to them, wrote letters for them, fed them, and cajoled them into getting up and trying harder. Gunner moved in and out of rooms, weaving through the beds and cots visiting soldiers, and accompanied those who were learning to walk with crutches or with missing legs or feet. He lay quietly with the sad and lonely, comforting them with his presence. He picked up and retrieved items for those who couldn't reach them and carried notes to and from staff members. The battles raged on, and the hospitals of Alexandria were bursting.

During March and April, the naval battles at Hampton Roads sent many injured Union sailors. Treated in field hospitals in Norfolk and Newport News, they were being hauled northward. By summer they arrived in Alexandria. Avery enjoyed the sailors, who loved telling their war tales. He wasn't sure how much was true, but he loved their stories. He encouraged them to retell the stories as good therapy.

Avery's favorite story was about the five ships involved in the now-famous battle that was being talked about everywhere. He saw the etchings of the battle in *Harper's Magazine* and listened to the sailors tell their story.

"Now the U.S. Navy had three battleships, yes sir, and one ironclad. On March 8, I was there, yes sir, the one Confederate ironclad ship—they call her the *Merrimack*—came steamin' down the Elizabeth River into Hampton Roads, bent on attacking the Union blockade."

"Oh, yeah, she thought she was something. That's for sure."

"Well, she was."

"Yeah, see, the blockade prevented supplies from reaching the southern states. The three Union Navy ships forming the blockade were already sunk or run aground by the *Merrimack*."

Boo, hiss. The sailors added the sound effects.

"Now then, the *Merrimack*, she was just skulking about waiting to attack and sink the U.S.S. *Minnesota,* which she'd run aground in shallows," explained a sailor.

"She thought so!" the sailors proclaimed with much animation and whooping, booing and hissing.

"Right, right, but . . . oh, she hadn't seen the *Monitor.* She's the U.S. Navy's ironclad, you know." The sailors cheered and whooped.

"Have you seen the *Monitor*?" they asked everyone listening. Then they'd give a low whistle, helping the imaginations to visualize such a wondrous ship.

"The *Monitor,* there she came out of hiding from around the battleship and chugged herself right into the fracas. Ah ha!" Avery mimed this part, acting out the ship sneaking around, to the great joy of the sailors.

"You shoulda been there; it was somethin' to see, all right! And she got off the first shot too." The Union sailors were especially proud of that and cheered the storytellers.

"Yes, sir, the first shot was ours!"

The story went that after four and half hours of steady fire, the *Merrimack* had to withdraw because of the falling tides. Neither side was damaged.

"The ironclad is here to stay," the sailors concluded.

"A whole new battle with them, like nothing you ain't never saw before."

Since he heard the same stories over and over, Avery was convinced that most of it was probably true. The part that was true for him was that the Union had lost four hundred and nine sailors. The Confederacy had lost twenty-four. Several of the Union's wounded were right here. Most had sustained serious burns when their wooden battleships burned. They were a long way from healed.

Avery requested that Dr. Simpson send couriers to find every beekeeper in the city. They would need lots of honey to make salves for their burns. Patriotic beekeepers arrived with crocks of honey that very week, and Avery spent considerable time preparing salves and ointments and teaching the other doctors to use and apply the honey as his mother had taught him.

The battles raged on all summer and were coming closer and closer to the nation's capitol and Richmond. The Union set its goals on Richmond; the Confederacy set its goals on Washington. Avery read newspaper accounts to the patients, who were hungry for news of the battles they'd left.

"Did we win?" they asked him. Most of the news for the Union soldiers wasn't good. "Did we win?" He wished he could answer yes. But the Union was taking a beating. He tried to give them other things to think about and offered riddles and puzzles to occupy them. Gunner came to play and distract them from the thoughts of the battles they were losing.

The voices of the angry citizens of Alexandria were finally heard, and in August, Lincoln appointed a military governor to restore order to Alexandria. President Lincoln himself would come and inspect the city to see it restored to order, the government promised. The military governor, General John P. Slough, set and enforced curfews, outlawed whiskey, and jailed anyone found in violation. Unruly soldiers were all returned to their camps. Alexandria quieted down and became once again a safe city for residents albeit under martial law, a city of war.

CHAPTER TWENTY-THREE

AN UNKNOWN SOLDIER

Avery and Gunner were processing a small group of invalids just arrived from the field. They were in various stages of despair and neglect. Avery couldn't find any records for some of them. One lay face down with his head totally bandaged. Avery tried to talk to him, but his face was buried in the blanket.

"Poor man must be smothering," Avery diagnosed. The patient was unable to lift or turn his head and was completely at the mercy of those handling him. Without any medical records, it was difficult to determine why he needed to lay on his face in the first place. He apparently couldn't speak.

"Orderly, I need a hand," he called to anyone who might be listening. In an eye blink Claire was at his side. He noticed that her scarf, holding the red curls away from her face, was drenched in sweat. Her apron was bloodstained. But she always wore a smile.

"How may I help you, Doctor?" she asked competently. *Where did she come from*, Avery wondered, *and how'd she get here so fast? She just pops up everywhere.*

"See if you can devise a way for this man to breathe. Until I figure out if he can lie on his back, he needs to be getting more air into his lungs. Keep his head still until I find out what his injuries are. This entire bunch seems to have arrived without any records. I'll see what else I can find out about him."

Claire surveyed the situation, told the orderly to wait, and she disappeared into the chaos of the hospital. When she returned, she was carrying two long poles used for emergency field litters and a large roll of bandages. In no time they had the soldier comfortable on a cot that they extended with the two poles. Between the two poles under the man's forehead and chin she tied strips of bandages, which held his head comfortably, while allowing his face to be free of the bed.

"There," she said. She picked up a *Harper's Magazine* and placed it on the floor under the man's face. His arms hung down, and she placed his hands on the magazine.

"There you go. Is there anything else we can get for you?" The man was silent. Claire and the orderly went separate ways to be useful somewhere else.

At the end of the day, Avery came back to see the man and was pleased to see him resting comfortably and breathing easily. He saw the opened *Harper's Magazine* on the floor.

"Well done, Claire," he murmured to himself.

At supper that evening, Avery bragged to Dr. and Mrs. Simpson about Claire's invention.

"We should remember it; it could be useful in other cases," suggested Avery, and the surgeon agreed. He'd compliment the nurse tomorrow, he told Avery.

Mrs. Simpson shared the happy news that General Keese and his regiment had returned to Alexandria from battle, and he'd join them on Sunday for dinner.

"Some of his men are at the hospital," Mrs. Simpson told them.

So Avery wasn't at all surprised the next day to see the general visiting in the hospital. Gunner was the first to see him arrive, and the happy dog weaved himself and his wagging tail through the first-floor crowd and across the yard to greet him.

"Well, well, it's Gunner. I must be in the right place then. Your buddy Avery must be here someplace. Where is he, Gunner?"

"Right behind you, sir," said Avery, smiling. "Good to see you, sir." The general walked with Avery, visited patients, joked and encouraged them, gave them war news, wrote letters, and played cards. In the late afternoon, he found Avery.

"Avery, uh, Doctor . . . I've been looking for one of my men. He's a new three-month recruit I picked up in Grafton on my way back from Ohio. I'm sure he was brought here, but I haven't seen him yet. He's Private McCorkle. Know of him?"

Avery thought about it. "I haven't seen that name anywhere, sir. I think I've seen all the patients here today."

"Well, if you should see his red head tell him Major General Keese wants to shake his hand."

"Oh, red haired is he?" asked Avery. The general rolled his eyes.

"And how!"

"Well, I've not seen any redheads except for our nurse Claire. She gets to know all the soldiers; we should ask her about him. And I'll see you on Sunday." Avery went back to work; the general went back to camp.

The next Sunday Mrs. Simpson had a lovely breakfast set out.

"All this for General Keese?" teased Avery.

"I just felt like a little celebration today, Avery. Yes, he's coming, and I also invited that nurse that you and Dr. Simpson go on about. Claire, I think her name is."

"Claire? Claire is coming here?" An alarm was going off. He felt his face flushing already. The girl left him feeling stupefied and awkward.

"Yes, she is coming along with us to church this morning, and then she'll stay for dinner. She seemed truly delighted to be invited; perhaps she's a bit homesick. I think we'll have a lovely time, don't you, Avery?"

He gulped. Mrs. Simpson busied herself with preparations for breakfast, church, dinner, and company. Avery decided he'd best be a good sport, get dressed, and go along. A knot was forming in his stomach.

"How is it that we can work together, but I can't talk to her, Gunner? What's wrong with me?" He was dreading this day.

It was a lovely fresh morning, and Claire looked stunning

in her green bonnet. Avery had never noticed before that her eyes were green. In fact he'd never noticed much about her at all. She was always . . . well, just Claire, everyone's favorite nurse. He usually avoided looking directly at her; she affected his concentration.

In the buggy on the way to church, she was full of bubbly conversation, and Mrs. Simpson seemed quite taken with her. She was very excited about going to church, she told Mrs. Simpson. She talked about church-related matters, which Avery didn't understand. He was feeling a little annoyed and left out at the moment. But at least he didn't have to talk to her. As always, he tried to listen intently and learn something new. But somehow when Claire was speaking, his mind got jumbled up, and he had trouble concentrating on what he might learn. Her eyes were as clear and green as a trout stream, and Avery caught himself staring. He didn't want to be rude or be caught looking, so he studied his shoes. He knew his face was turning red; he could feel it. *What is wrong with me? What is it about that girl that makes me so mixed up?* Avery was getting himself totally out of sorts; he was starting to feel a bit grumpy.

"This is the oldest parish in all of Virginia. It was established by George Washington himself in 1795," Mrs. Simpson told them. "It's Saint Mary's Church. George Washington was an Episcopalian, but he made the first contribution to build this one, and the chapel was built at the south end of the city. It was moved here to the center of the city later, oh, I think around 1810 or thereabouts."

When they walked inside, Claire was barely breathing. Avery looked around, and he too felt breathless. He'd never seen anything so beautiful. He didn't understand any of what was said or what anyone was doing, but he was captivated by the beauty of it all. He'd never seen a stained glass window before, and the sunlight reflecting through it captivated him.

Claire, kneeling and praying with the sunlit colors of the window falling across her like a rainbow, looked like an angel to Avery. He was enthralled. Claire and Mrs. Simpson both knelt to pray with folded hands. Claire's fingers were red and raw from the abuse of the harsh soap and water at the hospital. *I'll make her a salve for her hands.*

Back at home Dr. Simpson poured mugs of hot cider and said he'd like to propose a toast. Avery, General Keese, Claire, and Gunner all looked a little surprised and interested in what the occasion might be. Mrs. Simpson smiled smugly.

"I'm so glad we could all be here together today, all of us friends of Avery's. I'm proposing a toast to Avery today, to the next great surgeon, who's been accepted into the Medical College of Virginia in Richmond beginning next month. My dear Avery, you've achieved a perfect score on your entrance exams. The deans are quite impressed. Congratulations! Let's drink to Avery's matriculation."

"Hear! Hear!" they all said, and raised their mugs of cider in toast. Gunner put his paw on Avery's lap and barked his congratulations.

"Thanks, everyone." Avery felt his grin spreading across his face stretching from ear to ear. "I've been so busy at the hospital, I forgot all about having written the exam, and even forgot I was waiting to hear. I can hardly believe it—medical school!"

Claire was jubilant. "Oh, Avery, that's so wonderful, and aren't we all so proud of you. You'll be brilliant! And to have done so well on the exam, well, a bouquet of violets to you."

He felt pleased that she was happy for him, and he could tell she was sincere. He wondered if she'd miss him when he was gone. Not that he cared. Well, they'd gotten to be pretty good friends, he had to admit that. They enjoyed the pleasant dinner and conversation for much of the afternoon. *Maybe*, he mused, *I will miss her.*

"By the way, Nurse Claire, Avery tells me that you know most of the patients' names," said the general. "Most commendable in that there are so many and they come and go continually. I wonder if you've run across one of my men. He seems to have vanished in thin air. I was sure he was brought into Mansion House Hospital, but no one finds a record of him. Would you happen to have met a Private McCorkle?"

She glanced quickly at the officer. "No sir, no one by that

name at all. I'd remember that one. McCorkle is my family name. It's my mother's name from my Grandmother McCorkle. No, I'd surely remember that name."

"Well, if he shows his red head here, you'll know it's him. Oh, I apologize, Claire. No offense intended," he smiled.

"No offense taken, sir," the red-haired girl replied and smiled back. "Do you know the private's given name?"

"Not sure . . . well, not for certain. But, let me think . . . It might be Timothy. Yes, maybe Timothy. I collected him in Grafton."

"Timothy? Timothy McCorkle? Red-haired Timothy McCorkle? From Grafton?" Claire looked pale. "Would you all excuse me, please? I need to go, I . . . I need to get back to the hospital. Thank you kindly, Mrs. Simpson." Claire was fumbling in a very un-Claire way, Avery thought. Something had touched her off, he could see that. He'd never seen Claire floundering like this.

"Claire, wait, I'll go with you." Avery and Gunner could hardly keep up with her as she ran down the cobbled walk through the city, the bonnet ribbons blowing in the wind.

"Claire, what's this about? What's your rush?" he panted. "What're you doing? Will you tell me where we're going?"

"Don't ask so many questions, Avery," she spouted as she raced up the steps to the hospital through the door and into the melee of nurses and orderlies, the sick and the dying, the clang of bedpans, and the moaning of the miserable. She ran into the report room and began paging through the reports.

"Claire, what are you doing?" he demanded. He took her arms firmly in his hands. "Calm down and tell me, what—are—you—doing?"

"Avery, do you remember last week, the soldier with the bandages?"

"They all have bandages."

"The one I made the special head rest for? Where is he? They've moved him. Where is he? And more importantly, *who* is he?"

"He was one of the five who had no report. No one knows his name, and he's unable to speak. I don't know where he's been moved. Why?"

"Avery, I have to find him." He looked at her intently and decided not to question any more.

"Let me see those reports." He scanned them quickly looking for his own handwritten notes.

"Here it is. I know where he is; follow me." They ran up the stairs to the second floor to a large ward room that had been someone's ball room in its previous life.

"He's in the corner," Avery pointed.

Claire lay down on the floor directly under the soldier's face. The bandages covered every part of his face; only his eyes peered through openings in the bandages.

"What's your name, soldier?" The soldier's blank eyes stared, but he said nothing.

"Is your name Timothy? Are you Timothy McCorkle McDougal?" She touched his arm. He moved. He struggled to lift one hand a little and dropped it.

"I think you're Corky. Are you Corky? Are you a tater?" She held both his arms in her hands. The man stirred and seemed to be writhing within himself. She studied his face. Avery studied his body.

"Keep talking to him, Claire," Avery said softly. "Keep touching him." He watched the man's body move whenever she touched him.

"Corky, it's me, Claire. Can't you see me?" She picked up his limp hands and held them close to her. She pressed his hands to her lips and kissed them gently. She held them against her face. She closed her eyes and prayed. She felt softly falling wet drips on her face, like warm rain. She opened her eyes. The soldier's blank eyes were crying.

The next morning, Avery went to the hospital early to see Timothy McDougal. This was Claire's brother, the missing soldier of General Keese. He was known to his family as Corky, to his neighbors as Tater, to his commander, Private McCorkle. At the hospital he'd been known only by a bed number; now he had a name, Private Timothy McCorkle McDougal. Avery studied the report and talked to Timothy about his injuries. The soldier still hadn't spoken or made any response to indicate that he heard him.

He removed the fresh bandages from his head and checked the wounds, which were mostly on the back of his head and neck. He was missing an ear. He had a row of stitches across his forehead, which Avery could tell had been done hurriedly and carelessly. His hair had been shaved off in order to clean the wounds. He examined the lifeless, unseeing eyes. How temporary or how permanent, he couldn't tell. The one thing he did know was that Timothy McDougal would soon be on his way back to Kanawha, invalided. Then he remembered that the general said he wanted to shake the soldier's hand. Perhaps he would be decorated first and then invalided.

CHAPTER TWENTY-FOUR

MAIL CALL

The cooler breezes of September blew fresh air into the stuffy hospital rooms. Avery and Gunner received a letter from home. The letter told about the Congress at Wheeling and the constitution for the new State of West Virginia. Father and Clayton would soon be home. Clayton was studying law. The letter told about the new school for the Kanawha community meeting at the meeting house. Adults learning to read were coming to reading classes at the Bennett farm. Avery smiled as he imagined some of the adult neighbors sitting in his chair at his mother's table learning to read from a primer, exactly as he'd done. Thirty valley children attended the school, including nine from South Carolina. He could tell from the letter that their school was already a success.

He rubbed Gunner's head. "What a good thing Mother has done, eh, Gunner?"

His mother wrote they were all a bit nervous and concerned, because last month the Confederacy advanced into the Kanawha Valley to take the city of Charleston. There was a battle on the thirteenth day of September, and the Union forces withdrew across the Ohio River overnight, leaving the city of Charleston, West Virginia, in the hands of the Confederacy. This was news to Avery, terrifying news. This news was upsetting to hear and something to worry about. He chewed his lip and rubbed his head where it ached. He made a point of reading all the newspapers' accounts of *all* the battles from that day on.

He answered his mother's letter, congratulated her on her success, and told them that he'd be entering the Medical College of Virginia in a few weeks. He tried to fill them in on the details of his life, but he didn't want to give them any reason for worry about his safety, so he didn't mention the troop movement and battles around Richmond. He didn't mention the injured tater, in case tater Claire hadn't yet written home. He didn't mention Claire, because . . . he didn't want to. He looked forward to seeing them one day soon. He hoped the war would soon be over. He signed with love in his best handwriting. Father always said a man's signature should be legible and a matter of honor.

Avery spent many evening hours studying in Dr. Simpson's medical library. He consulted with any surgeon passing through any of the hospitals, but no one had any answers for Timothy McDougal. So Avery gathered volunteers, orderlies, and nurses together and explained his plan for Timothy.

"I want someone with the soldier for three hours every morning, every afternoon, and every evening. In between those hours, the patient must eat and rest. Someone needs to talk to him, rub him, and move his limbs constantly." Claire assured him that it would be done.

"When he goes to sleep, it should be because he's tired," said Avery. "Being tired and going to sleep is a good thing; going to sleep to escape, isn't." The nurses nodded; they understood. For the next few days, whenever Avery was on that floor, he saw nurses with Timothy, talking, reading, rubbing his back, moving his legs and arms.

"The poor man looks absolutely henpecked!" chuckled Avery. He examined Timothy every evening; and after about a week, he thought he detected some improvement. But Avery was noticing other things. His eyes had a bit more light; they looked more alert, more alive, Avery thought. He looked like any moment he could get up and walk away and be perfectly normal, but he wasn't able to do so. So far, all his wounds were healthy and not infected. He asked the volunteers to take the soldier outside and try to get him interested in doing something. Try to get him to speak.

At midday Avery saw Timothy and his crew of nurses under the trees throwing a ball to Gunner. They lifted his arm and helped him hold the ball. When Gunner returned with it, they placed the soldier's hand on Gunner's head.

Nearby Avery watched orderlies trying to carry large bundles of supplies into the back door, when the door was suddenly pushed open from the inside and the orderlies with all their bundles, crashed down the steps. Everyone in the yard jumped and looked. Some of the invalids, who were still shell-shocked, reacted with haste and fear. Everyone looked. Everyone except Timothy, who continued to try to throw and let go of the ball.

"He didn't hear that," Avery said out loud. He went to find Dr. Simpson and told him that blind Private McDougal was also deaf. Dr. Simpson looked sad and nodded.

Avery wrote a message to the general and sent a volunteer to take it to the camp. Later that week he received his reply: "Private McCorkle was with the artillery unit. They were behind a stone fence waiting for the enemy to approach across the corn field. When they began to load the cannon, before they could fire it, the cannon misfired. McCorkle saw what was about to happen and hurled himself onto the soldier who would've been hit when the cannon exploded. He was on top of the other soldier when the cannon blew. The explosion ripped open the back of McCorkle's head. The cut on the forehead, we think, was from falling on the cannon bed. Exploding cannons are a constant source of danger to the artillery platoons and frequently leave the soldiers with hearing loss. More often, leave them dead."

"The head wound probably damaged the part of the brain that manages limb movement. Is there anything we can do about that? Not much is known about the mysteries of the brain. Do you know of any specialists?" Avery asked Dr. Simpson.

The doctor was impressed with Avery's deductions. He thought there was a surgeon in Philadelphia who might be able to help Timothy. Avery sent the doctor in Philadelphia a letter, asking for his opinion in Timothy's case.

The surgeon's reply came the week Avery was leaving for Richmond. Dr. Simpson arranged for two orderlies to accompany McDougal to Philadelphia. "I will pray for you, Timothy," Avery said. He was very excited the morning he was leaving for Richmond.

"Oh, my goodness how I will miss you both, but I'm so happy and excited for you," Mrs. Simpson fussed and fretted, and hugged the boy and the dog.

"I'm nervous, Gunner, how about you? On the one hand, I can hardly wait to start medical school. On the other hand, the idea of going into Richmond, a city under Confederate occupation, is kind of frightening. Maybe they'll know us for Yankees and shoot us right in the street." The idea terrified him. He'd have a lot of time to pray, he thought, one hundred miles' worth of time.

"I'll carry medical bags in plain sight on both sides and wear my yellow medical insignia where it can always be seen; you need to wear your cape, too, Gunner." He hoped the rebels respected that. Gunner twisted around and shook, getting his cape comfortable.

Avery packed his few articles of clothing, some books, his journal, and his medical supplies. He had duty pay in a little wallet. "I wonder if we can use this money in a Confederate city?" He shoved the wallet into the knapsack.

He'd planned to take the railroad part of the way, change trains, and go to Washington, D.C. From there, he, Fan, and Gunner would make their way to Richmond. Avery wished he could ride in the stable car with them. The straw sure smelled better than the train car. He thought his plan was complete until Dr. Simpson gave Avery something different to think about.

"Are you sure you want to take Fan to Richmond, Avery? You know that she won't be secure and could end up sequestered into the Confederate Army." Dr. Simpson was right. He'd read in the paper that there were hardly any horses, cows, or anything else of value left in the hands of the people of Richmond. And so he decided to leave Fan with Dr. Simpson in Leon's care. Fan would be safer in Alexandria with the Simpsons' groom.

The train was hot and crowded, and the seats were just as scratchy as Avery had remembered. Soldiers were laughing and joking and passing a flask.

"Hey, Doc," one of them called out to Avery. "Where you headed? Wherever it is, they'll be needing you! Hey, did you hear they're building a mountain in Richmond?" All the soldiers and some other men joined in with noisy voices. "Yeh, that's right, that's what I heard too." "Guess how they're doing it?"

Avery shrugged, not really interested.

"It's a hill of arms and legs from all the amputations over the summer." The men laughed and slapped each other on the back, enjoying their joke. Avery smirked to be friendly, but he didn't think it was funny. He visited with a quiet businessman for a while who told him the summer of 1862 had been dreadful months of turmoil for Richmond.

"The Seven Days Battle all around the Richmond area caused residents to leave home," he told Avery. "If they left, they risked having their homes confiscated by the Confederacy. If they stayed, likely they'd starve. Best you be careful there, young fella. Richmond's not the classy city it once was. Well, good luck to you," he said shaking hands. "They can use another doctor, that's for sure. Take care now." They parted company on the train platform. The businessman went to collect his luggage. Avery went to let Gunner out of the livestock car.

The next day Avery gathered his acceptance letters and reported to the Medical College of Virginia. The class of 1863 convened in the lecture hall to be welcomed and informed.

"Gentlemen, welcome. This will be your home for two terms, that is to say, thirteen months. Your course of study involves lectures and practical experience. Then you will write your exams and be awarded medical degrees as surgeons. You must work hard, and we wish you good luck. The war won't shut down our school," the director asserted. "Nor will the war penetrate these walls from within. Here we are neither Union nor Confederacy. We are gentlemen of the medical profession." Avery was relieved to hear that soldiers of both sides were treated equally and no student could "take sides."

The dean spoke next. "You are expected to keep your bodies and souls clean and your minds sharp and diligent. Insubordination, laziness, or theft won't be tolerated. Women are never allowed in the dormitories, and you are expected to be in your rooms by dark unless you're on duty at the hospital. Everyone has a desk and a bookshelf as well as a footlocker in which to house your clothing and materials. Welcome." Avery looked around. He was the youngest student in the room.

The medical director, Mr. James McCaw, a close personal friend of Dr. Simpson, then announced, "On a lighter note I'd like to announce that your class has a mascot. May I introduce Gunner, a medical corpsman with a year's experience as a corpsman? Gunner."

Gunner pranced forward wearing his cape. The thirty students in their class laughed and applauded. Gunner made the rounds, getting acquainted, sniffing, shaking hands, and making friends. The students were delighted to make his acquaintance, and as far as Gunner was concerned, they were already best friends. So Avery and Gunner began their lives as students at the Medical College of Virginia in Richmond.

CHAPTER TWENTY-FIVE

RICHMOND

The days and nights passed quickly. For the most part, his life on campus was pleasant. The four roommates were diligent and quiet, and they were all working hard at the same goal—to become surgeons. Avery enjoyed the lectures and created stacks of notes that he referred to regularly. He felt capable at work, and his opinions were respected. He shared advice on the treatment of wounds and his mother's use of herbs. He assisted in surgery and tried to learn something new every day. He was so busy he hardly had time to notice how much he'd grown.

A student named Tilman seemed to have taken an instant dislike to Avery. When they passed in the hallways, Tilman never made the little sidestep adjustment and instead would plow his shoulder into Avery and his roommates.

"Aw, maybe teacher's pet should go to the infirmary and cry."

It took every bit of Avery's discipline to keep from popping Tilman in the nose. Where did he get the notion that he was a teacher's pet? He worked as hard as anyone. Tilman made snide remarks in stage whispers about the "rich kids from the north," referring to Avery and his roommates. They'd all heard him, but they had no idea why he felt this way. None of them were rich and none of them were from the North. They tried to ignore him, knowing he was trying to goad them into a fight, which could get them all expelled. There wasn't much time to dwell on Tilman.

The Chimborazo Confederate Hospital was a huge complex, and the students learned early to work as a team.

One morning Avery was preparing to leave his room for the day. He washed, dressed, ate, fed Gunner, and filled his doctor's bag and his knapsack. His routine was methodical; it never varied. The last thing to go into the footlocker at night was the flannel packet of his grandfather's surgical instruments. The last thing to go into his doctor's bag in the morning was that same packet. This morning it wasn't there. He panicked, and he mumbled. He emptied the trunk; he talked to himself. He tossed the cover off his neatly made bed; he grumbled, and then he spouted louder. No one had ever seen Avery flustered like this. He was obviously upset, and he kicked the contents of his locker on the floor.

"Where is it? Where could it be? I know it was here."

"What is it, Avery?"

"What did you lose?"

"It's my instruments, my surgical instruments in the flannel packet. My grandfather's instruments. Where are they? They should be here!"

His roommates were sympathetic and offered to help look for them, but no one had seen them. Avery paced, trying to remember if he'd done anything different in his routine last night.

Gunner pawed the trunk. He sniffed inside and around the edges; he began to whine. He sniffed around the floor.

"What is it, Gunner? You got the scent? Find it, Gunner." The others watched in amazement as Gunner's nose went to the floor. With his tail high in the air and waving, he began to make a circle in the room, nose snuffling along on the floor. He made a little groan and followed his nose to the desk belonging to Jones, one of the roommates. He sniffed around the chair and followed his nose up the back of the chair until his paws were on the desk, then he sniffed into the air. The owner of the desk watched him and followed him to the desk. He followed Gunner's gaze up to his bookshelf. Gunner whined and stared at the bookshelf.

"My compendium! It's gone," Jones cried. "I bought it with the last bit of my book money. It's rare; I can't replace it.

It's gone! Someone has taken it; it was here last evening when I studied."

"Wait a minute," said Jack. "Someone took Jones' medical compendium? Someone took your instruments?" They all looked stunned.

"Stolen?"

Gunner was back on the floor. He made the loop through the room, sniffed through the door and into the hall, following the scent of an intruder's steps.

"Find him, Gunner," Avery said quietly. All four student doctors followed Gunner down the hall.

Jones said, "I'm going to get our hall purser. I think we're going to need him." He ran down the hallway in the other direction.

Gunner pawed under a room door. He scratched around the door, sniffing loudly. He began to paw the door wildly just as the purser arrived with Jones. The purser knocked on the door.

"Open up, please. It's Dr. Stevens, hall purser here. Open the door," he called loudly.

The door cracked open.

"What do you want?" said Tilman. Gunner shot through the purser's legs, threw the door open, and ran into the room, nose to the floor. He followed the track to the trash basket next to one of the desks.

"Get your dog out of here, Bennett," Tilman growled. Gunner scratched at the basket and barked. The purser picked up the basket and dumped the contents on the floor. All the wadded study papers tumbled out, followed by a wad of hair from a recent haircut, followed by a metallic clink and the thud of a heavy book.

"My compendium," gasped Jones, lunging toward the mess on the floor.

"These are my grandfather's surgical instruments." Avery anxiously picked up the flannel packet and dusted off the barbered hair. He untied the flannel wrap and showed it to the purser, who nodded.

"This your desk, Mr. Tilman?" the purser asked.

"What if it is?"

"Pack your belongings. Wait right here and don't leave this room. The dean will arrive shortly, and you'll be escorted from the campus."

Before Tilman could say or do anything but sputter, they all left, shutting the door behind them.

"Sorry about that, doctors. Jones, I hope your compendium isn't damaged. I know they are dear and hard to come by. Glad you found your grandfather's instruments, Bennett. Thanks, Gunner!" He rubbed the dog's head. Avery and his roommates scratched Gunner's back and ears and hugged his neck.

Avery stood staring at Tilman's door. "Why'd he do that? Why'd he throw away his chance to be a doctor? Why do you think he'd do that?"

The others shrugged. "Who knows why people steal things? Glad we got our things back."

"I don't care what they do with Tilman. He's just a common thief as far as I can see," said Edward.

"But he wanted to be a doctor," Avery said quietly, mostly to himself.

Jones said, "He threw away that opportunity when he chose to become a thief. Don't feel sorry for him. Gunner, I hope the cook has a good supper planned tonight because I'm sharing mine with you, old boy! Thank you, thank you, thank you!" The roommates shook hands with the purser and hurried to leave for class. Avery wondered, once again, how he could get along without Gunner.

It was later that day Avery learned that the Confederate occupation of Charleston, West Virginia, was over. More than twelve thousand Union troops were headed for Charleston, and the Confederate troops were withdrawing. Little damage had been done in the Kanawha Valley. He took a deep breath and relaxed for the first time in weeks and uttered a thankful prayer. But all around the campus, the clouds of artillery smoke gathered and hung most of the time. Avery couldn't remember when he last saw a really clear day. Some days the sun itself seemed to be hidden beneath the fog of cannon fire. The Union was advancing. How much longer? How long before the battle would be right here in Richmond? Would they have a Christmas holiday this year?

Avery wrote a short letter to Dr. and Mrs. Simpson telling them he'd be arriving for seven days over Christmas and was anxious to see them again. He wrote a note to Claire telling her that Gunner was going to be at the Simpsons' over Christmas, in case she wished to visit the dog. With two days for travel, the five days would go quickly in Alexandria.

Mrs. Simpson hung boughs of greenery tied together using her embroidery threads. Avery was amused to see it tied to the front door when he arrived.

"Not quite as pretty as ribbon, but it'll work," she explained. "Textile mills that make such things as ribbons and nonessential luxuries are being used for war essentials. There's little of anything for sale that's nonmilitary these days. Food's not plentiful, but thank goodness some is still available." She chatted merrily, happy to have her favorite boarders back at home.

It disturbed Avery to see that here in Alexandria, even the unflappable Mrs. Simpson didn't have sugar for her tea; she only drank real coffee on Sundays. And there was no ribbon for her holiday decorations.

"Further south," Dr. Simpson said, "in Confederacy occupied cities and states, materials and food are dire. There's little of anything left. The Union's blockade is working. Nothing finds its way south either by sea or rail. The Confederate Army might be winning the battles, but the Southland is starving." Avery gave a little shudder.

"On the college campus where we're neutral and discussion of the war is banned, it's easy to forget that civilians also suffer," Avery told Dr. Simpson. "Most of the news we get on campus about the war comes from our patients. We can't respond or get involved with discussions at the risk of being expelled."

"There are no sides in medicine, that's for sure, Avery," Dr. Simpson said, and Mrs. Simpson nodded in agreement.

"It'll all be over soon," she added. Avery thought she

Richmond

sounded quite confident about that. He wasn't sure he agreed. One day Avery and Gunner visited Mansion House Hospital and gave a hand with the volunteer work.

"What can I do to help you, nurse?"

"Well now, this is a turnabout, isn't it?" Claire laughed. "Gunner, how good to see you, you ol' hound dog nurse. It's good to see you both." He thought she seemed really happy to see him.

On that cold December afternoon, Avery watched in fascination as Claire directed her little band of nurses in the side yard. *She is obviously in charge,* thought Avery, *and why is that a surprise?* He used to think she was bossy. Now he thought she was a competent leader.

The nurses had seven ambulatory patients lined up under the trees. The men scratched furiously. The nurses were cutting their hair. They snipped, sheared, and scrubbed the soldiers' scalps with lye soap. The soldiers complained loudly, rubbed their burning eyes, and shivered in the cold. They yelped and hopped doing the "louse dance," as the nurses rinsed their irritated scalps with kerosene to treat their head lice. He smelled the kerosene in the air and remembered how rough and raw Claire's hands had been last summer. He needed to make her a salve for her hands. He'd forgotten to do that.

On one of the five busy days of his vacation, Dr. Simpson asked Avery to reorganize the Mansion House Hospital as he'd talked about. So Avery gathered the staff of orderlies, volunteers, nurses, and doctors under the trees in the side yard and explained the plan. Avery's reorganization plan was greeted glumly. It sounded like a lot of extra work for everybody. No one believed the extra work would make a difference to the patients, and he could tell that the staff wasn't happy about this. Dr. Simpson assured him they would follow the plan in spite of their grumbling. No one, including Avery, really knew how much difference any of this would make. Perhaps it was just extra work. He hoped not.

A few days later, the staff's reports began to filter back to Dr. Simpson. The staff noticed a significant reduction of flies and gnats, which made their entire workplace more comfortable. They liked confining the smell of the camphor lamps to the top floor, giving relief to the rest of the hospital. The surgeons discovered fewer amputations were necessary. Staff found they had more time and energy since they weren't scurrying up and down the stairs continuously between floors. The outdoor area was more pleasant without the irritating flies and gnats; and with the daily removal of limbs and bandages, it just smelled better. Dr. Simpson was so happy with Avery's reorganization plan that he sent a note to the deans at the college, telling them that they might wish to listen to the boy's ideas.

No one had any idea why these simple changes made any difference. Some thought it was a useless waste of time, but those who really studied the entire picture saw that these simple procedures really did make a difference. Avery was pleased.

CHAPTER TWENTY-SIX

CHRISTMAS IN ALEXANDRIA

Christmas Day was a beautiful sunny day. There had been only a little snow so far this winter of '62; and though it was cold, it was pleasant. Mrs. Simpson noticed the blooms on the hellebores were way ahead of schedule, and several of her herbs were already replenishing in the garden.

They began Christmas morning at sunup, and Avery helped Mrs. Simpson set up the breakfast. Where she'd managed to find all of the ingredients was a mystery to Avery, but he was in too good a mood to wonder about it for long.

General Keese wouldn't be joining them today. His regiment was on duty and perhaps even involved in battle today. Claire would be arriving soon for breakfast and church. Gunner, Avery was sure, would be very happy about that.

"Here she is," crooned Mrs. Simpson, going to the door. When the bell clanged, Gunner was the first to reach the door. Avery stood back and watched as Mrs. Simpson gave Claire a cheek kiss and invited her in. Mrs. Simpson took her cape and gloves, and Claire removed her bonnet. The red curls escaped, and there she stood smiling at him.

He could think of nothing to say. He nodded his head lamely, and said, "A good Christmas to you, Claire." He wondered if he said it out loud or if it was only said in his head.

He sat next to Claire in church and was again overwhelmed with the beauty and solemnity. The smell of the incense, the gleam of the candles, the joy of his friends were all of great interest to Avery. He liked how the colored glass made rainbows over the congregation. The translucent colors shimmered on the walls and seemed to call out to him. He could almost feel the color. He knew that sometime he'd study more about this. For now, he enjoyed being enveloped in the peacefulness, in the soft colorful rays from the sun, sitting next to his good friends.

The afternoon was joy filled, and talk didn't involve the war or the sick and dying. Some of Mrs. Simpson's neighbors stopped in and brought a little Christmas cake. "Wherever did they find it?" Mr. Simpson whispered.

They gathered around Mrs. Simpson's little piano and sang some Christmas songs. They were learning a new song, written by Julia Ward Howe called "The Battle Hymn of the Republic." Mrs. Simpson was learning to play the melody. It was a favorite song of the Union soldiers at the Mansion House Hospital, Dr. Simpson told Avery. Claire knew most of the words already. Avery hadn't heard it before. His patients in Richmond sang about going home to Dixie.

Late in the afternoon, Mrs. Simpson brought out a little basket. It was filled with small items wrapped in paper. She handed out a little package for everyone.

Avery brought out his knapsack and removed gifts he brought. He had pipe tobacco for the doctor, a package of flower seeds for Mrs. Simpson, and a great bone for Gunner.

He shyly passed a tiny package to Claire. When he saw it at the apothecary shop in Richmond, he wanted it for her, but now it looked so small. *Maybe she won't like it. Maybe it's not a good gift for a girl, after all. What do girls like?* He began to feel a little panic. How, he wondered, could he feel so sure of himself at the hospital and be so unsure where this girl was concerned? Why did she do this to him?

When she opened it up, her face was all surprise and pleasure; Avery relaxed a bit. *Maybe she does like it.*

"Oh look!" she showed it to Mrs. Simpson. "Avery, these are the most beautiful little embroidery scissors I've ever seen.

Wherever did you find them?" she said.

The tiny silver scissors looked like a heron. The feathers and the eyes had been worked into the silver by a silversmith. The thin blades, the beak of the heron, were razor sharp and pointed. She held them in her palm, and it was obvious that the little scissors pleased her.

Though flooded with relief, he was annoyed at himself and thought he was certainly taking this whole gift-giving detail much too seriously. *They are just a pair of scissors. She's just a friend. What would it matter if she didn't like it?*

"Do you embroider?" Mrs. Simpson asked her.

"My mam tried to teach me, and I would love to do it well, but I'm too clumsy. I always thought that when I was a lady, it would just come to me. Do you think it will?"

"Oh, my dear, Claire," Mrs. Simpson laughed, "you're already very much a lady. You must come by and let me teach you. It's a wonderful relaxation and a good skill to have. I'd love to teach you."

"I would love to learn, Mrs. Simpson. I'll definitely hold you to that."

At the end of the day, Dr. Simpson suggested to Avery that he should escort the nurse back to her quarters. Avery wasn't sure what escorting entailed. He hoped it didn't mean that he would have to talk to her. The girl made him tongue-tied and awkward, and he could think of nothing to say. *What do girls talk about?*

As the sun was setting, Avery walked Claire back to the nurses' quarters and her dormitory. In spite of himself, they talked and laughed; all too soon the walk ended. Avery and Gunner jogged back to the Simpsons' in a very gay mood. He realized, with much surprise, that he'd actually talked to her and he'd enjoyed it. He didn't remember what they'd talked about.

Two days later as the snow began to fall heavily on the ground, Avery and Gunner returned to Richmond. When they reported back to the Medical College of Virginia in Richmond and to the Chimborazo Confederate Hospital, Avery discovered that in seven days many of his patients were gone and several new ones had arrived.

Some of the new ones had seen action at the Battle of Fredericksburg earlier in the month. Lasting for five days, the battle was being celebrated in this hospital with jubilance and renewed vigor for the war. Avery hoped this wasn't where General Keese had been, for the Union troops had suffered terrible casualties. His Confederate patients were all eager to share their experiences and heroics. Some who'd sustained injury, proclaimed, "It was worth it!" "We really gave it to them Yanks!"

According to these veterans, the victory had been so one-sided that Burnside asked Lee for a truce in order to tend his wounded. Lee graciously granted the truce, and the next day the Federal forces collected their injured and dead and retreated. The Richmond newspaper reported that it wasn't a battle; it was butchery. The hospitalized soldiers were cheering at Chimborazo. Avery knew that Mansion House Hospital patients weren't cheering. Claire would be bolstering their spirits, and surgery would go on for days.

Gunner was better at remaining neutral. Avery watched his busy dog making the rounds to the enjoyment and comfort of the battle-weary soldiers. Gunner didn't know Confederate from Union, nor did he care.

"We should all be more like Gunner," Avery said. "Then maybe this war would be over."

It seemed to Avery that the one thing that was equal as the year came to an end was that everyone was suffering in one way or another. Sitting with a sick patient who wanted to write a letter home, Avery listened to the words and wrote them down for the sick soldier. He tried to write to his own family later that night. He wished them all good health in the new year. He told them about Christmas Day at the Simpsons' and a bit about the hospital. He wished he could tell them when the war would be over. But, no, he didn't have much to say; nothing had really changed since his last letter. He imagined them sitting, reading, talking in front of the fireplace; he tried to picture himself there. He felt a bit melancholy; he was missing them all. Perhaps this was homesickness. *There isn't a cure for that, is there?* Maybe he'd write a letter to Claire.

He sat up with a patient late into the night on the last day of the year.

"What time is it?" asked the soldier wearily. Avery glanced at the large clock on the canvas wall. Some days the clock was slow; some days it was fast. He wasn't sure, but he answered, "I think it's 1863 . . . five minutes ago." The soldier died shortly after that. *He was probably the first fatality of this brand new year,* thought Avery as he covered the man. He filled out his report and called for an orderly to remove the soldier, a nurse to make up the bed, and a corpsman to move in another patient needing a bed. He put on his coat, and he and Gunner went to the dormitory to go to bed.

In the dark of the night, the war continued on as 1862 came to a close, and 1863 came in on the morning train.

WHAT'S TRUE
AND WHAT ISN'T

Everything you read about the government, the congressmen, the Constitutional Convention, the formation of the State of West Virginia, and the onset of the Civil War are all historical fact. Marauders, deserters, and the Home Guard are also real.

The geography, the Staunton-Turnpike, and the rail lines are accurate according to historic maps. The almanac says it rained all summer in 1861.

The Battle of Philippi Bridge was real; there were no injuries, no fatalities, and no shots were fired. This was one of the first confrontations of the war, and one of the few that the Union won.

The picnic was typical of many battles, and the hot-air balloon and the photographer were real parts of the Civil War. Thaddeus Lowe, Mathew Brady, and Mr. Sullivan were all real people.

The Mansion House Hospital of Alexandria existed and can be seen today as the Carlyle House Museum. You may also visit the Hollywood Cemetery. The Mansion House Hospital is depicted in the book as closely real to the original, with a few sidesteps into my imagination. It, too, is based on museum information and old photographs.

Medicines used by Avery, his mother, and the hospitals are all documented. Some are still in use today, and others are part of modern compounds.

The Quakers are actually quite diverse in their beliefs and practices. Some Quakers surely could have served the war efforts as Avery and his family did; they could have believed and lived in their communities as the Bennetts are portrayed. Such groups were known to exist in Virginia after the Civil War, and it is possible that they were in the Kanawha Valley in the 1860s.

Quaker women throughout American history have been strong women who spoke out on important issues such as intolerance, equality, bigotry, and slavery.

The rainbow trout that Avery caught became, decades later, the official state fish of West Virginia, and the timber rattlers are alive and well in the mountains today.

The descriptions of all the cities during the war are based on historical fact, carefully researched. Alexandria today offers an "old towne" tour covering many of the blocks in our story.

Many changes were occurring during this time: changes in the warfare (ironclad ships), attitudes toward women (working as nurses), the disruptions of their way of life (antislavery), and shortages of supplies and food. These changes are all part of Avery's story, and he, too, was changing.

The Medical College of Virginia in Richmond was the only medical college in the country that did not close during the war. That's a fact.

The Chimborazo Confederate Army Hospital did exist and is accurately depicted, based on photos of the tent wards and museum documents. Dr. James McCraw was really in charge.

The answer to Avery's father's 1861 Christmas riddle is *a cow*.

Children would have enjoyed Moravian ginger cookies, and Mrs. Mikesell's recipe might have read like this:

MORAVIAN GINGER COOKIES

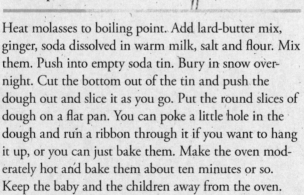

1 cup molasses
1 tablespoon ginger
1/2 cup lard and butter mixed
1 tablespoon soda
2 1/2 cups flour
2 tablespoons warm milk
1/4 teaspoon cinnamon
1 teaspoon salt
1/4 teaspoon clove

Heat molasses to boiling point. Add lard-butter mix, ginger, soda dissolved in warm milk, salt and flour. Mix them. Push into empty soda tin. Bury in snow overnight. Cut the bottom out of the tin and push the dough out and slice it as you go. Put the round slices of dough on a flat pan. You can poke a little hole in the dough and run a ribbon through it if you want to hang it up, or you can just bake them. Make the oven moderately hot and bake them about ten minutes or so. Keep the baby and the children away from the oven.